THE MORALIST OF THE ALPHABET STREETS

Marsh "exhibits the same sophistication and wit that marked her 1988 debut." —*The New York Times*

"a literary masterpiece" —*The Midwest Book Review*

"sylphlike, winningly punctilious...Marsh writes so gracefully and has an acute (if inwardly spiraling) sense of humor." —Ralph Novak in *People*

"a New Yorker who writes like a tar heel and thus gives us this funny novel filled with exuberant tragic characters." —*Library Journal*

"Like Frankie (in Carson McCuller's *The Member of the Wedding*) Marsh's Meredith views the world in a wistful, touchingly idiosyncratic way, while always standing apart from the action she so beautifully renders." —Meg Wolitzer in the *Chicago Tribune*

"Outstanding...This is a book of exceptional warmth and grace. It is entirely engaging in all parts and lingers with the resonance of its deeper messages, presented to us like a platter of fresh fruit on a humid, storm-lowering day." —*Small Press Review*

"packs a punch that is wry and witty as well as, yes, uplifting." —*Metroland* (Albany)

"Marsh's prose is so direct and unfussy that its powerful emotional wallop surprises." —*City Pages* (Minneapolis)

"delightful and surprising." —*Winston-Salem Journal* (North Carolina)

"Splashingly saucy, benevolently brashy, endlessly edgy, devilishly delightful and ravishingly readable." —*The Macon Beacon* (Georgia)

D0595771

"Fabienne Marsh is a skilled and compassionate writer, who has created complex characters who looks with more than usual perceptiveness into the convoluted nature of family and neighborhood relationships." —*Rocky Mountain News* (Colorado)

"In a warm, richly drawn coming-of-age story, a delightfully wry observant 18-year-old with a fondness for frankness and affection-tinged cynicism learns about love and mortality during one important summer." —*Booklist*, Editor's Choice

"Marsh has written a wonderful book. There's a little wisdom in every sentence and laughter on every page. I cried until I laughed." —Michael Lewis, author of *Liar's Poker*

TRANSATLANTIC AND COAST-TO-COAST ACCLAIM FOR FABIENNE MARSH'S FIRST NOVEL AND NATIONAL BESTSELLER LONG DISTANCES

"What an impressive debut...Great charm and power and the ability to breathe life into each character. LONG DISTANCES deserves every hyperbole it receives. The reviewer would attempt to add an ornate and spectacular one here, but he is too impa- tient to get back and re-read the book." —*Orange Country Register* (California)

"witty...a charming debut." —*Time Out* (London)

"Strong, wise and entertaining...Marsh's wit is devilish. Her compassion great." —*Boston Herald*

"compulsively readable" —*Chicago Tribune*

"A fresh spin on (the) first novel..." —*The New York Times Book Review*

"Fabienne Marsh uses a respected literary form, the epistolary, seldom seen in contemporary works, with skill, grace and deft effectiveness; she creates a real and likeable family..." —*Pittsburgh Press*

"What makes the novel fascinating is...the technique...By the end of the novel, I felt like a small town postal worker snooping through mail, piecing together my own version of this unfolding drama." —*Charlotte Observer (North Carolina)*

"very funny, touching, and sad all at once" —James Atlas

"A SUPERB FEAT OF MAGIC, A MASTERFUL NOVEL." —*San Mateo Times* (California)

"A surprisingly accomplished effort for a first-time author..." —*ALA Booklist*

"This book is pure magic. I loved reading every page of it. *Long Distances* is the debut of a superb new writer." —Pat Conroy, author of *The Prince of Tides*

"This book is made up of letters and postcards many of which are so accurate they make your skin crawl." —*The Observer* (London)

Literary Editor's Selection (*The Times*, London) A Book-of-the-Month-Club Alternate Selection Washington Square Press Paperback.

JULIETTE, RISING

Juliette, Rising

Fabienne Marsh

Windtree
Press

Publisher's Note: This is a work of fiction. Names, characters, places, and incidents are a product of the author's imagination. Locales and public names are sometimes used for atmospheric purposes. Any resemblance to actual people, living or dead, or to businesses, companies, events, institutions, or locales is completely coincidental.

Poem "This Be the Verse" by Philip Larkin. Copyright 1971 by Philip Larkin. Reprinted by permission of Faber & Faber.

Excerpt from "Musée des Beaux Arts." Copyright © 1940 by W.H. Auden, renewed. Reprinted by permission of Curtis Brown, Ltd.

Excerpt from *Labyrinths* by Jorge Luis Borges. Reprinted by permission of Penguin Books Ltd. A Penguin Random House company.

Jacket Design by Mladen Bozic

Juliette Rising / Fabienne Marsh. – 1st ed.

Print ISBN 978-1-952447-52-5

Ebook ISBN 978-1-952447-51-8

For my son, my daughter
and my brother,
with love

ACKNOWLEDGMENTS

I would like to thank

Kevin Hinchey, Julian Krainin, Dustin Lane, Anne Lebreton,
Maggie Lynch, Diana Maychick Foote, Henry Peyroux,
Michelle Labrie Ripple, Gwen Sullivan and Frederic Thys for
their unwavering support;

and the Malaga Cove Library for a haven in which to write.

CONTENTS

Letter to the Afterlife

Dear Mom,

Someone must set something down. I am the
only one left.

I feel wholly unfit as the guardian of our family's
history. I cannot bear to look at the hundreds of
pictures and home movies, the jottings in the
margins of books, and the watercolors from
family vacations, which fill Dad's sketchbooks.

The world is a different place.
It feels huge and empty.
A lot has happened since you've been gone.

Over the years, you asked me to document the
ordinariness of my life. You claimed it made you
laugh. So here it is: part email-to-the-afterlife
and part companion for the living.

Your death coincided with Hurricane Jeanne.
Because you'd been christened Jeanne, the hurricane— strange as this may sound —became a
rare source of comfort.
The world outside was violent. I was in sync
with the world's elemental forces of rage and
despair—war, suicide bombers, pandemics,
tsunamis, financial ruin, and nature's perennial
reminder of her power, hurricanes.

I hope that if I have inherited anything from you
and Dad, it is your ability to focus on the absurdity of daily life long enough to tickle out laughter, passion, and hope.

Your request, for a fallen Catholic like me,
lingers like church incense, or like one of those
haunting imperatives I used to hear in mass:

Do this in memory of me.

All My Love,
Juliette

Mother

I like a look of Agony,
Because I know it's true —
Men do not sham Convulsion,
Nor simulate, a Throe —

Emily Dickinson

Do you suppose our country would have been settled
If the pioneers had worried about being lonely?

Carl Dennis, 'Invitation.'

1

GO WEST

I moved to Oregon after the father of my children blew up our brownstone on West 97th Street in New York City. I had no doubt the move would be better for our children, though I worried they would never have a normal childhood.

Our intermediate move was to the New York City suburb of Larchmont, where my best friend, Pat, and her husband owned an apartment. After my son, Sam, spent all his time on the playground burying dead animals and my daughter, Grace, was the only girl in her first-grade class not invited to an American Girl birthday party, I accepted a teaching job in Portland.

After that same American Girl's mother, Crystal, said there was no room for Grace in Brownies, I told Pat I'd lost patience with the mothers in Larchmont. Crystal, who named her daughter after a cheese, was the head of a book club that assigned short, bestselling non-fiction titles like *What to Say to God When You Get to Heaven* and *How to Talk to Your Children about Their*

Inheritance. After Crystal made our book club listen to Brie read her reflections on Barbies, ladybugs, and unicorns, she looked at me with a vision of her child's future glory blazing in her irises.

"What do you think?" she asked.

"Wonderful," I said, determined to get my heartbroken daughter into Brownies.

"No, I mean, *really*. You teach at that fancy private school that's a feeder school for Yale."

Before I could answer, Crystal stated that Brie was a genius. The other mothers vigorously agreed, but not before noting that their children also had exceptional talents. I did not tell them that as both a fourth-grade teacher and a mother in this era of 21st century parenting, there was virtually nothing I had not witnessed. With all the in-utero Mozart, Suzuki Method, Jump-Start apps, Kumon, Sudoku and soy snacks, there should not be a dummy in the bunch.

I was never invited back because I wondered (aloud) if there could be so many geniuses in the world, let alone a disproportionate number of them both in the state of New York and affiliated with our Larchmont book club.

"Crystal's a cunt," Pat said, with the irredeemable vulgarity she manages to control in front of Sam and Grace. "You did the right thing."

Conversations with Mothers of Geniuses (MOGs) like Crystal, as well as better job offers, and the aggressive (and in our case, violent) nature of life back East were reasons enough to move. What's more, our financial future looked bleak, and we were not alone. After The Great Recession, suicides were at an all-time high and parents behaved like Flaubert's *Pere Goriot,* a man who so loved his daughter he moved to smaller and smaller rooms in Madame Vauquer's boarding house in order to finance her lavish lifestyle. In today's terms, this corresponds to the sacrifices parents make to fund their children's obscenely expensive college education.

The glue that prevented me from moving were my friends and family, many of whom had nursed us through a hideous custody battle that, consistent with statistics from the U.S. Census, landed us squarely in the ranks of poor families headed by single mothers.

Two years later, I confess to pining for some of the very things that drove me West.

People out here are so protein-powder, low-carb healthy and laid back that I miss my wine-swigging, cigarette-sneaking, bipolar friends in New York.

Today, Pat called to tell me that *The New York Times* had an article about a bereavement group she wants me to attend. "They're doing very interesting work," she said.

Pat claims to have jurisdiction over my grieving process. According to Pat, who is in mourning herself, I am not grieving properly. I never hit Denial, Anger, Bargaining, Depression, and Acceptance at either the correct stages or at the right time. And forget about experiencing them in the proper order, assuming I experience them *at all.*

"I think the Bereavers are in your neck of the woods," she says.

"Which neck would that be?" I ask.

"Tryon Creek State Park. Isn't that near Portland?"

I am always giving Pat geography lessons, as I do for all New Yorkers. I begin with Lewis and Clark, The Louisiana Territory, and Thomas Jefferson. In the Pacific Northwest, the expedition's goal was to learn where the continent ended. When I get carried away about Lewis's noble dog, Seaman, Sacagawea, and the difficult winter at Fort Clatsop, Pat always interrupts.

"I really don't give a rat's ass about the Indians or the explorers."

So I ask her what she does care about.

"Everybody's dying," she says.

And here we go again. Because what Pat says is true. Four years ago, Pat's husband died of ALS. One year later, she lost her mother to breast cancer and three months ago, her Pomeranian rescue died of congestive heart failure.

"Tryon Creek State Park is very close to Lewis and Clark College."

"Isn't that where you teach?"

"No."

"Close enough. The group meets every Wednesday."

"I hate groups."

"You'll like this one."

"I don't 'share.'"

"I'll go with you," she said.

Pat knows that I will do *anything* to get her to visit Oregon, so I tell her I will think about it.

"What about your new boyfriend?"

"What about him?"

"Won't he miss you?"

"He travels a lot."

I ask because Pat likes men and they like her. She goes to daily spin classes, invoking the envy of women who work a great deal harder to keep figures that are far less girlish than Pat's. Though she is in her forties and nursed her beloved husband through a relentlessly grueling disease, Pat's still got it. At five feet ten inches, she beats me by an inch. Men find her raspy voice sexy even (or especially) when tossing out vulgarities that could make her Pomeranian's nipples blush.

My voice is soft and low, *sans* rasp, and I cuss only when the occasion warrants. Eyes are a point of pride for both of us: hers are huge, expressive, and espresso-colored; mine are large and hazel. When the sun catches Pat's wavy, auburn-colored hair, it flashes like copper (she prefers my caramel blonde mane with gold highlights). She looks like an equestrian, with long legs and a fragile yet tenacious grace (I'm curvier and trip constantly over my students' backpacks). When Pat was a child, she owned a horse named Happy. It took her a full year of intensive therapy to forgive her mother for selling Happy while she was in college. But how she loved *my* mother, Jeanne!

The thing I am finding is that I only want to be around people who loved the people I have lost.

"Are you asking if Bill will miss me?" Pat asks nonchalantly.

After her Pomeranian died, Pat took comfort in writing to one of her old Connecticut boyfriends. She'd had a torrid affair with him at Fairfield University, after he saved her from flunking statistics, and was seeking to renew their short but deliciously illicit Jesuit-school relationship. This common history is something that

Pat and I cherish. Actually, it's stronger than that; we crave it. So much so that when we find people with a similar past, we prolong friendships and romances beyond their natural expiration dates. We have lost the elasticity necessary to form new relationships the way other women lose bone density. Because our closest friends and relatives live either very far away or in the Afterlife, we have had to get through the day with complete strangers.

"*Il faut s'ameubler,*" I can hear my mother say, which is the French metaphorically existential way of saying that when your house is emptying out, you have to rearrange and/or surround yourself with new furniture —no doubt it works *much* better in French. On some days, I have that wintery, desolate feeling that I am simply killing time, which is not how passionate people want to live. Pat says that we are honing the skills required for success in an assisted living facility, where studies show friendly, flexible social elders who drink wine fare best. But deep down, Pat and I are terrified because, though we excel at polishing off a bottle of wine with dinner, we might not end up in the same Sunrise assisted living location. What's more, we do not play Bingo and we do not wish to dance the Hokey Pokey in water fitness class for health and socialization.

When we visited nursing homes for my father, we saw elderly people with so much history trapped inside them, happening elsewhere, with people they missed. They did not play Bingo either, *nor* did they smile when the Girl Scouts sang Christmas carols. To be fair, a few vacant stares came alive after a tone-deaf Santa sang "Jingle Bells," but only because Pat moaned, "Christ, would somebody give Santa a blow job and shut him up!"

My father died at home. Thank God.

Bill's first email set the tone for their long-distance romance: "I still carry a small flame for you in my dotage." These daily *frissons* via text messages have helped her move forward with her life.

So have her animal rescue projects.

Pat has no children and her only child, the deceased Pomeranian, began what she calls her Brigitte Bardot phase. "I devoted my youth to men," Pat says, quoting Bardot. "I devote my best years to animals. Very *chic*," she adds. "Like your French mommy."

Pat has no idea how much I dream about my French mother and my French grandmother.

During the day, I lead the life of a single, working mother, summoning up the machinery for survival. At night, I descend into the darkness and anxiety of an active, traumatized mind. When I dream, I do not want to wake up. I do not want to leave those I love. I feel literally torn from the dream. I smolder like a rocket booster, scorched by re-entry. I have trouble participating in the day. I might be going through my daily routine, but it's as if I am living in another time. I plod on, hunting and gathering, getting and spending, but I carry an entirely different reality into my day. I need strength. I need coffee. I need affection. I need medication. I need love. I need understanding. I need a belief in something outside of myself. I need to know that I am not alone. I need to know that I have not lost my mind. *I need to know that my beautiful, sweet children (and all the students I teach) will not be fucked up for the* rest of their lives because of what adults have put them through.

I am startled by the specificity of my dreams. Last night, for instance: I am in Paris. I am ten.

I cannot find my grandmother's home on the Rue de Berne, near the Place de L'Europe. I take the wrong street—Amsterdam, Budapest, Madrid or Constantinople—crossing what seems like a huge plaza, with Danger de Mort! *posted on the enormous fence above the tracks. Below me, dozens of rails merge like a cinched corset. The throb of transportation rattles the bridge under my feet. Under the hangar at the Gare St. Lazare, train after train stands ready for departure—Geneva, Berlin or, within the region, Charentes-Maritimes. The whistle sounds, the Depart! is announced, and by the time the train passes near my Grandmother's apartment, I hear the soft rhythmic shuffle of the wheels gaining speed.*

I am lost. I am lonely.

The smells of Paris combine in varying amounts: dampness, dust, dog droppings, bus fumes and, inside the stone courtyards, mold. A Hollywood chewing gum wrapper holds the promise of mint. The confiserie has a baptismal display with dragées, sugarcoated almonds, smooth as clam shells eroded by the surf, and hard as marble. I stop to buy my mother the small, silver ones, which look like beads of mercury.

When I arrive at my grandmother's house, my feet are hot, swollen, and tired. I am wearing patent leather Mary Janes.

She is not home.

I had to sell my parents' home just as Pat sold her mother's home. I would have sold our marital home on West 97th Street had Nick not blown it up with himself inside, having kept my name off the deed to the property.

"I despised Nick," Pat confided to me during the memorial service his parents had organized. "He was a calculating, lying, cheating, bottom-feeding, asset-hiding, sociopathic Ivy League scumbag." There was very little room for anyone else's rage as Pat snatched up every existing share of Nick-loathing stock on the free market.

Nor is there any point in discussing Nick with anybody other than Pat because even well-meaning friends and family members ask rational questions like, "Didn't you see the warning signs?" And the answer is no. I did not. It was impossible to see any warning signs because when I happily kept Nick's world aloft, he worshipped me and the children. After he lost his job and started to unravel, the paranoid detritus of Nick's brilliant mind re-organized itself, collecting injustices and focusing on his new Enemy #1—me.

I was raised not to speak ill of the dead, yet I do not mourn the departed with equal power or intensity. In Nick's case, I am heartbroken that my children lost their father (and our puppy—I have no words), but I do not mourn Nick as a wife. The cruelty was so profound that any sun flares in my heart have long been extinguished.

"All narcissistic sociopaths are alike," Pat said, with Tolstoyan authority while binge watching *The Jinx*.

"They're all like Nick or Robert Durst. They destroy their family, their friends, and themselves."

Only those who've been on the receiving end of their lack of empathy can fathom the sudden and chilling emotional shift from buttery sunshine to the darkness of, well, *winter is coming.*

Pat tells me that one of the recommended exercises for the Bereavement Group is to write remembrances, poetry, or letters, which make me really NOT want to attend. But the truth is: That is exactly what I have been doing every night because I have tried everything and nothing else helps – not even classics like C.S Lewis's *A Grief Observed.* I am composing messages almost like prayers. They might be messages-in-a-bottle, or emails to the Afterlife, but they are communiqués I am compelled to write down. I feel a bit like the scientists who search for extraterrestrial life. All those beams going out; only static coming in.

Letter to the Afterlife

Dear Dad,

Here's where we left off.
Mom died. By that time, your short-term
memory loss was acute, which turned out to be a
blessing.

You died eight months later. One month after
your funeral, we moved in with Pat after Nick
lost his job and blew up our home. The only
lagniappe for history buffs like you (and the City

of New York) were the thousands of artifacts unearthed in the crater left by the blast; among them, John Stuyvesant's wig curler.

Sam and Grace are okay, but just okay. I never speak ill of their father. Tomorrow we fly to Los Angeles to visit Grandpa Chola and Grandma Kristina. My heart is breaking because I would rather be taking them to visit you and Mom.

I promised Mom that one day I would write a book "instead of just reading them." I want to write the book I've been trying to find. I want the book to help others who are suffering.

This book will not be about Nick or the divorce. I loved being married and, somehow, I still love men.

I love you, Juliette

My children make it both impractical and impossible for me to lose my sanity, though they cope with grief in ways that sometimes break my heart. Sam makes gravestones in clay class. He asks me birth and death dates, to be as precise as any stone carver. Grace paints rocks from the garden and leaves them on my pillow. She worries too much about comforting me. Her words reflect the received language of eulogy: In Loving Memory, Rest in Peace, Grandpa. Sacred Father. Beloved Grandmother and Great Grandmother.

Letter to the Afterlife

Chere Grandmere,

I can smell garlic while you cook *poulet chasseur*
at 8 Rue de Berne. I sit on your chaise longue,
asking you about the paintings on the walls and
the provenance of unusual objects—a silver hook
for lace-up boots and the pair of wooden
crutches I found in the closet.

Do you remember when we all visited the
church Van Gogh had painted in *Auvers-sur-Oise?*
Everything in the town, including the church,
looked gray and flat. The tourists would look at
the church on the postcard, with its undulating
cobalt sky and its spire swimming piously
towards the light, then they would glance at the
actual Auvers sky—pewter that day—and shift
their gaze back to the very church Van Gogh had
painted, a sour gray Gothic.

"This is *it?*" They all seemed disappointed.

I miss you and I miss our trips with Mom and
Dad. The world looks as gray and flat as Auvers
these days and I don't seem to be able to see it or
paint it any other way.

I wonder if you are saddened by your daughter's arrival so soon after you settled in. I suppose it would have been far worse if her arrival had preceded yours.

I think about you constantly, though I grieve for my parents far more than I do for you. After all, 101 is a stunning achievement.

Bisous,
Juliette

2

LOVE IS IN THE AIR

I am trying to pack. I should say, I am trying to unpack all the sharp items that magically appear in my son's backpack. They sound off alarms, which I do not need at airports, as I invariably get stopped because my kids and I don't match. I have blonde hair, hazel eyes, and fair skin. They have enormous brown eyes and skin the color of amber.

WHO CARES? We are ALL from Africa!

Except, African roots and genetics aside, the practical result is that we're never selected for the random TSA pre-check. Airport authorities often think I'm the nanny or the kidnapper. They do not want to revisit my fourth-grade lesson plan, "Introduction to Genetics," with Punnett squares. If they did, I could demonstrate how a mutt like me was genetically obliterated by Nick's very pure line of descent from India, via Grandpa. Love conquers all except when your husband resembles a handsome version of the 9/11 terrorist who took flight lessons in Minnesota. Nick was tall and slim with sensual features, chestnut eyes, walnut skin and a healthy shock of blue-black hair.

While I complete this routine pre-screening for LAX, the final hours with Grandpa Chola and Grandma Kristina are stressful. Sam and Grace have displaced the carpet cover in their grandparents' living room and have failed to respond to Grandpa's "Not to move!" command no fewer than one dozen times. Grandpa Gayen, who was nicknamed Chola by the children in loving protest for all the chickpea dishes they refused to eat, once possessed a gentle sense of humor. Kristina, who met Jay Gayen in Los Angeles as an exchange student from Germany, had a winning sparkle. Her sparkle and his humor were extinguished after the loss of their son.

The beige wall-to-wall carpet was not the issue. The cheap wool area rug on top of the wall-to-wall is the one they are trying to keep new. Grandma Kristina made a beautiful cotton fabric cover for the rug. That same day, she sewed a cover for their bed cover, a cover for the chair in their bedroom, and a cover for the bench in front of their bed. The *piece de resistance* was an embroidered cover for the sewing machine, from which all covers were created, in this blizzard of fabric creativity.

I am irritated because I don't know of many widowed ex-wives/ex daughters-in-law who travel to Yorba Linda, California to make sure the grandchildren pay regular visits to their out-of-state grandparents.

And, of course, the real issue has nothing to do with fabric and everything to do with the fabric of our lives.

Nick is the common thread, yet the unspoken rule is that we must never discuss him.

Grandma and Grandpa, who love Sam and Grace very much, have channeled their anger and grief over our divorce and Nick's death into highly systematic projects like shredding documents, overly zealous cleaning projects, and recently, homemade fabric covers for just about everything in their house.

Chola and Kristina have mastered the art of portion control for their broken, fearful hearts. They stuff the wailing inward, divide it into smaller, more manageable portions, scoop it into plastic, seal-tight containers, then stack them in the freezer. Each vessel is then pulled out on its designated memorial day, allowing time for its contents to thaw.

Too-much fabric, too-many carpets, and entirely too-little spontaneity in Grandpa Chola's world made me especially touchy when it came to taking off my shoes in the security line at Terminal 1 of the Los Angeles Airport.

I have been through the x-ray machine so many times that I can practically recite its serial number. I know that my shoes are buzz-free and that shoe removal is optional. I wore them because they are my buzz-free traveling shoes.

"Take your shoes off," the gatekeeper of the x-ray said.

"They don't buzz," I said.

"I'm asking you to take your shoes off," she repeated.

The twentysomething Special Forces X-Ray Agent wanted to teach me a lesson. Her instrument of humiliation was the wand. So while my children were trying to lift their backpacks onto the conveyer belt, she started doing a breast exam. The wand was overly sensitive and beeping like crazy.

"We need a wand calibration on machine two!"

She must have been five feet in heels, but she yelled like a drill sergeant.

While they worked on the wand, she started the hand thing. She was about to do the crotch thing when I demanded a private cabana.

"We've got a request for a private screening!"

Hundreds of irritated travelers gave me a collective evil eye and I don't blame them.

The agent makes my children take off their shoes and looks disapprovingly when Sam comes through the x-ray and performs his skateboard slide finish over what he perceived was a rail.

Grace burst into tears when a grandfatherly agent threw Grace's American Girl doll, Kaya, facedown.

"She'll suffocate," Grace said.

On the other side of the conveyer belt, a handsome man in his early forties appeared from an Employees Only door. He took one look at Grace and began administering CPR to Kaya of the Nez Perce tribe. Grace erupted into laughter, making me realize that I'd been holding my breath.

Behind a navy-blue curtain on rods and rings, X-ray Lady poked and prodded until finally I muttered, "Why don't you throw in a free mammogram?"

I was immediately led to a small white room in the airport office. Other than the three chairs we occupied, there was a table, on which someone had left a well-thumbed Bible.

I took this as a sign and composed an apology for my unholy behavior, thumbing a text to Pat.

Made REALLY stupid comment at airport security and they pulled us aside. Any ideas!?

Grace was drawing flowers on her Miss Kitty notepad. Sam was reading his *Essential Spiderman* comics. I was having one of those flat, depressing days. Nothing I could attribute directly to grief. The kind of day that will happen independent of circumstance. Inside me, in the vicinity of my heart, everything felt heavy, structurally unsound, and on the verge of collapsing. On days like today, there never seems to be enough oxygen. This is the kind of day many people experience every day. The kind of day that is unacceptable to me. The kind of day which makes me think of my father. "A ten razor-blader," he would say. I was looking at my children and thinking how amazing they were; by the ages of nine and eight, they had coped with more death and dislocation than most Americans experience in an entire lifetime.

"Hey guys? I'm sorry about this."

"It's okay, Mom," Sam said.

"They weren't very gentle with Kaya," Grace added.

My children will never know how simple travel used to be when I was their age. My mother would send me off to Paris on Pan Am. Alone. The takeoff had me on the edge of my seat— New York traffic, city lights — ascending into the ink of night. Eight hours later, an orange-raspberry dawn, followed by a roaring descent through the grey drizzle over Charles de Gaulle

Airport. Wings and a deck of cards from a Barbie doll stewardess were my only diversions.

I had lost track of time when the same tall man with the elegant walk, the beautiful smile, and the eyes of glacier blue we'd seen during the American Girl doll's mouth-to-mouth walked in. He spotted the Bible on the table, took it, and said he would be right back. "Some people can't board without them."

The only thing I had wanted from my Father was his Bible. He had never been religious, but toward the end, he read it every night. Before that, he had requested that Grandpa Chola send him the Kama Sutra. His dentist sent him the Talmud. He went to the library for the Bhagavad Gita and the Koran.

In the margins of Genesis 17:11 he had written, "Beginning of Circumcision!"

In Jethro 18, I had read "Jethro teaches Moses Management!"

In Numbers 28:3, he had fumed "An unforgiving Lord who LOVES animal sacrifice!"

In the first book of Samuel 13:13, he had wondered "What did Saul do wrong??"

Regarding Paul on charity, he wrote "Beautiful!"

In I Corinthians: 13 and I Corinthians: 15, he scribbled (and I wonder if he believed it) "The Death of Death."

In Numbers 21:5 (*for there is not bread, neither is there any water; and our soul loatheth this light bread*), he commented, "They never stop bitching!"

By the time Kaya's rescuer returned, Grace and I

were thumb-wrestling and Sam was playing Minecraft. This conditioned reflex occurs every time Sam suspects an adult conversation is likely to go on indefinitely.

"You're putting me in a tough position," the man began, then he smiled broadly and waved at the kids.

Grace used Kaya's hand to wave back.

"I'm sorry," I said respectfully. I grew further dispirited when my phone buzzed and I glanced down at Pat's text.

Bill would know, but I can't get through.

I was beginning to worry that we would miss our flight. "I stupidly suggested," I whispered, drawing close enough to smell Old Spice, "that if the security staff insists on x-raying women in front of their children, they might consider some health benefits to the procedure at the same time."

I wasn't being entirely glib. The wait had unnerved me. It reminded me of all the hours I had spent in an ice-cold waiting room, waiting for my parents' physicians.

I apologized for wasting the security officer's time and confessed that I was concerned we would miss our flight back to Portland.

"I liked your suggestion," he said, "and we had another issue that's been resolved." He handed me a note: *We just updated our No-Fly list.*

A stab of anger hit me cleanly in the heart. Nick's first move had been to pull the children's passports and obtain an *ex parte* hearing claiming that I was a flight risk and would kidnap the children.

"Can we go now?" Sam sighed.

"Yes, Sam, we can," I said with tremendous resolve, slipping my phone into my carry-on bag and helping the children re-pack and zip up their overstuffed backpacks.

It was occurring to me that this man was neither just a bin man, nor was he Grace's personal American Girl physician.

"I'm headed toward your gate," he said, glancing at Grace's backpack, on which was clamped every possible expression of passion for an eight-year-old: sour apple ChapStick, jewel stickers, a miniature pony, and a diamond ring one inch in diameter. "Do you like Claire's as much as I do?" he asked, referring to the accessory store conceived and dedicated to small humans carrying a pink chromosome.

I confess to feeling safe and utterly charmed by this man – so much so that I began to feel the stirring of something very strange, yet familiar. I can only compare it to the rush I felt during my year in London when Michael Rolland surprised me with a deep, stolen kiss in the movie theater after Al Pacino took Ellen Barkin against the wall in *Sea of Love*.

Had my children not been present, I might have said something suggestive. This is highly unlike me and I do not know what brought it on. The airport was cold and icy-white with LED lighting. This manly man was towering over me. I wanted to flick off the lights, jump up, lock my legs around his waist, and pin him down against the small table in the middle of the interrogation room. Ferocious attraction takes you by surprise when you have not had good sex in eight years. In this famished state, I was disgusted to admit to something I would never act on–fantasizing about sex with a complete stranger. Despite my vacuum attraction to this man with his unimpeachably smoldering exterior, I kept my distance.

"Spiderman's my favorite," he said to Sam.

"Spidey is totally awesome," Sam concurred.

As we made our way down the main concourse, the airport official addressed me privately. "You'll have to be a little bit more patient at the airport. We take flight risk very seriously and 9/11 is the day airport security changed forever."

As we approached the gate, my outrage fueled a longing to defend myself. "My flight risk status was the bogus vestige of a frivolous charge." Nick's pre-emptive strike in court succeeded because I had never received notice of the *ex parte* hearing.

I shielded my mouth with one hand so the kids could not hear. "He filed for divorce and served papers at my school the day before winter break. My mother and grandmother had just died. My father was dying."

I was breathless and stopped talking to secure his gaze. When he turned toward me with a look I read as guardedly sympathetic, I resumed. "I was commuting to work from my parents' house, taking care of my father and the kids."

We were walking so fast that I turned back to see Sam and Grace tumbling forward to catch up.

"My lawyer said that he had pulled the perfect stunt to get full custody. 'Nothing left for her, here, Your Honor,' Nick told the judge." My voice caught. "'Her father's ill and her French mother died.' He declared me a flight risk because I had dual citizenship."

"I'm aware of that," he interrupted.

I longed to talk to him. On September 11th, I had been visiting Minnesota. I explained that I had lived in New York City for so many years that I had felt local. In the land of 11,000 lakes, I had walked around Lake Harriet that day; the next day, I had circled Lake Calhoun. On the third day, around Lake of the Isles. People were talking about what they always talked about: their children, their jobs, their spouses, and their friends. I had been eavesdropping, waiting for someone to say "Pentagon," poised for someone to say "World Trade" or "White House," but no one did.

I was still talking as he waved us through security. My hourglass with him was running out of sand. I was determined to tell him that I had stepped inside a few churches in Minnesota on the morning of September 11th. Empty.

I had called Pat. We remembered Philippe Petit and his miraculous tightrope walk from the North to South towers, *that were no more.* I had called every person I knew out East. I could not get through.

One week later, Minnesota received the official call from its churches. You could not get a place in a pew.

Where have you all been? I wanted to say.

I had never felt so alone.

Dozens of passengers were already lined up to board our flight. I had resigned myself to the fact that I would never again see this fellow traveler.

Sam stepped over and shook his hand.

"You're an outstanding young man," the man said.

Grace flashed him a peace sign. "Claire's," she said.

"It's a date," he said.

"Thanks for putting a human face on Airport Security," I said. Impulsively, I asked for his name, but "FINAL BOARDING CALL FOR FLIGHT 206 TO PORTLAND, OREGON" was blaring over the PA system. I think I heard Bob. Bob Cummings.

"I'm Juliette." I grabbed his hand. I don't know if he heard me.

I felt uneasy after the plane took off, embarrassed that I had poured my heart out to a stranger. I was suddenly irritated by his parting words to my daughter: "It's a date."

I hate it when adults do that.

I hate it when adults make promises to kids so casually, things that kids remember forever, in that *cross-your-heart-hope-to-die* way.

I never do that to my students.

I know I need to calm down, but I'm so mercurial these days. What if Mr. Airport Security was toying with our feelings? Right now, I need to trust that nobody toys with people uttering honest words, spoken from the heart.

When the plane leveled off, I stared at the coastline near Topanga Canyon and a riptide of grief pulled me under. I turned my face towards the window so that Sam and Grace could not see. Interrupted conversations make me sad. They are a searing reminder of the ultimate in aborted communication, the one that comes with the finality of death.

Letter to the Afterlife

Dearest Mother,

Last night you hopped into a cab in New York City. The driver leered at me, then locked all the doors and sped away. I saw you look back with a frantic expression. You knew you'd been snatched by a madman. You knew you would never come back. You were not ready to die.

I have had this dream at least once a week since you died. Each time, I feel utterly helpless as I watch you go, which is exactly how I felt the night you really died–in the hospital, with all your vital signs going from their gloriously strong neon zigs and zags to flatline on a black screen. Your heart stopped. My heart pounded and has been broken ever since.

The cab ride was your final voyage–a headless horseman careening and kidnapping you to into the Afterlife.

I am so frightened by my dream that I need to know you're okay. I'm asking you for proof of life from the other side.

I miss you terribly.

Love,
Juliette

I do not wish to further upset my mother by including my memories of her graphic and grotesque ending. She did not experience the good death for which everyone now prepares, as if death is as organized or as pleasantly reliable as an IRA distribution. My mother's death was quick, sudden, and horrifying. She had been in perfect health, ministering to my father's prodigious caregiving needs, complaining only of a mild pain in her side. One week later, she was diagnosed with ovarian cancer. Four weeks to the day, she was dead.

I remember every waking second of every day of those few weeks, from diagnosis to burial. I would give anything to forget.

3

PLAY BALL

Lucas from Extreme Sports Club invited me out to Jamba Juice. It's a big deal out here, where everything is EXTREME. When they introduce a new drink, it's a date event for people like Lucas.

Lucas is very fit. He mountain bikes and uses all sorts of menacing machines at our state-of-the-art health club. By the pool, while I sip my Oregon Pinot Gris, he'll down another 100% whey protein Bavarian chocolate shake. If Lucas is being really naughty, he'll chew Turkey Jerky while drinking diet chocolate soda and read about high-altitude training in Nike's "Oregon Project." Every morning, his vitamin cocktail includes fish oil for vascular health and hemodilators to open his blood cells. His scientifically tested cell supplement enhances MUSCLE SIZE and STRENGTH and CELL VOLUME and OSMOSIS. And just in case you're thinking of cashing in on all this, know that this cellular voodoo is PROTECTED BY PATENT.

I am wary about Jamba-juicing with Lucas because

he's in the Kumbaya stage of divorce. On the upside, he is a swarthy, dark-haired environmental lawyer who reads biographies about the Founding Fathers and John Muir on the treadmill. He insists one day he will write a book. On the downside, Lucas thinks that he and his ex-wife-to-be, Carol, along with their lawyer and marital therapist, will sit around the campfire making Divorce S'mores together—this graham cracker is for you, this Hershey bar is for me. Do you prefer your marshmallows gooey or flambé?

The only problem is that Kumbaya and his team do not have access to the lady's locker room. I wish I had known Carol in the early stages of my divorce. She is extremely well informed about Notices of Motion and Orders to Show Cause and familiar with chapter and verse of family law that no one becomes intimate with unless they are premeditating and/or possess a first-rate criminal mind. So when Lucas shares his travails with me on the treadmill and says that he yearns to Jamba with me now that they have separated, I am anxious, though I accept his invitation.

"What can I get you?" Lucas asked.

"Lime Sublime. What are you getting?"

"I don't know yet." He smiled, scanning my body in high-resolution. "What's your squeeze of the day?"

"My what?"

"Sorry, I was talking to the smoothie guru."

"Hey, Lucas! How's it going?" Guru was at the cash register waiting to take our order.

"Great," he said. "I always ask about the special but get the same thing."

"Two shots. One wheat grass and one orange ginger cayenne?"

Lucas gave him the thumbs up.

"That sounds revolting," I said. The line was getting longer. I was craving anything remotely unhealthy. "Do you mind ordering me a three-cheese Bistro sandwich?"

We found a table outside next to the door, and Lucas got right to the point.

"I'm extremely attracted to you." He looked up imploringly. When the sun hit his green eyes, I saw tiny specks of copper.

A customer wedged the door open, extending the line outside. The blenders roared with decibel levels rivaling those of a jackhammer.

"Thank you," I said, "but I want to be clear from the outset—"

"Absolutely!"

"I like your kids. I hope you like mine."

"I do!"

"I think Sam and Grace enjoy Joey and Mia's company."

"They had lots of fun at the climbing wall last week."

"Thank you for that."

"My pleasure."

"I'm up for doing things with the kids—"

"Me, too–"

"But that's *all* right now."

He looked disappointed and stared down at his clasped hands.

"LUCAS SCHELL!"

"I think our order's ready," I said.

Lucas was so focused on delivering my sandwich and smoothie that he dropped his one-ounce shots in the process. They fell on the table; the light breeze blew the green and orange liquids into the form of a tree, reminding me of the straw drawings my students did in class.

"I'll take care of it," I said, placing my hand gently on his shoulder. I returned with paper towels and two free refills from my new best friend, the smoothie guru. "Go easy on him," SG said. "He's a nice guy."

Lucas threw back his wheatgrass as if it were a shot of tequila.

"Lucas?" He looked at me with an intensity that made me feel edible. "You're newly separated with a long road ahead of you, especially if you put the kids first. Which you should."

"I'm sorry," he said. "You've been through a lot and you've told me the half of it. It's just that I really like you and I haven't felt this way in a long time."

He buried his head in his hands and moaned.

"What's the matter!?"

"Carol and I haven't had sex in two years!"

I burst out laughing at the absurd turn in our conversation and lowered my voice after noticing the man who'd been in line behind Lucas smiling.

"Right now, you're a fetid swamp of boiling hormones..."

"See!" he laughed. "Carol can't even talk like that. She doesn't read and we have nothing in common."

"What did you have in common when you married?"

"We wanted kids," he said solemnly. "We had the same values and went to the same church."

"Reason enough for most people to get married and stay married."

"Well, it's not enough for me. She never shuts up and I'm not interested in anything she talks about."

"What does she talk about?"

"Her new line of therapeutic creams."

I could not think of anything to say, other than to ask if he'd made sure the creams and their packaging were safe for the environment.

"I like you, Juliette," he whispered. "You're sexy, interesting, and funny. And because I'd rather see you than not enjoy your company, I'm going to accept your terms. I'll do stuff with you and the kids. For now."

The deafening blenders came to my rescue.

Two days later, Carol mounted the treadmill next to me.

"Will you be joining us for the Triathlon?" she asked me.

You would not know that she is the Senior Vice President of SusieQ Cosmetics. Her face is tan and leathery and she bleaches her teeth.

"No thank you," I said. I smiled and pointed to the panel on my treadmill. It's on the lowest setting. "I don't jog."

She reached over and punched one of the buttons. "You do now." She smiled. The rubber mat spun so fast that I fell off.

"What are you doing!?" Lucas appeared from the weight room, shouting at Carol.

When I waved him away, he stood like a cave man robbed of his club.

"You seem to like Juliette so much. She might as well train with us."

"I don't train."

"Do you spin?"

"No."

"Do you climb?"

"No."

"Do you lap?"

"No."

"Besides teaching fourth graders how to blow up volcanoes with baking soda, what do you do?"

"Yoga with Valinda."

A few minutes later, while Lucas was collecting their children in Kid's Club, Carol sat at the club's juice bar, sipping her Strawberry Tsunami. As I headed for the yoga studio, I could feel her eyes trained on my Nike logo, as if putting my heart in the crosshairs of her sniper. I decided to give up discussing Thomas Jefferson or the founder of the Sierra Club with Lucas because he is living in the shadow of Vesuvius. Vesuvius will explode. Vesuvius will roll over him slowly, burning him with molten lava, petrifying him and all his assets in her wake.

In New York City, when I was single, my friends would always ask, "Where did he take you?"

I would say the Odeon. They would say, *Cool.*

I would say Carnegie Deli. They would say, *Too cheap.*

I would say River Café. They would say, *Romantic.*

I would say Trattoria Dell 'Arte. They would say, *Cultured*.

So they ask the same question about Lucas. I say, he's in the midst of a divorce, with one boy, Joey, who is a fourth-grade friend of Sam's, and an adopted girl, Mia, who is in Grace's third-grade class. I say he's an environmental lawyer. Then I say, he took me to Jamba Juice for a Lime Sublime. They say, *You're kidding, right?*

I don't know what will become of Lucas and me. After what I've been through, I am probably seeking a less complicated, decent man with a big heart. At the health club, Lucas is working with Carl Fortuna, a cancer survivor, to help bring Carl's own Lance-Armstrong-type story to film. My children love to rock climb with Joey and his daughter, Mia. Lucas is also handsome and affectionate. His green eyes are deeply set under a high, honest forehead and his lips are full and sensual. I feel as if I am writing those dog intros for Best in Show. *Decent. Loyal. A great athlete and a stalwart companion. This is Sporting Group Labrador #204. Lucas Schell handled by Carol Schell.*

Dating habits out West are vastly different from twenty-something dating habits back East.

For starters, I am forty-something. In my case, this makes me in better shape than I was two decades ago. My face used to be very round, with large hazel eyes, but now my cheekbones are showing. Pat says that I have "superb bone structure." "But you could do a lot more," she says, appraising me like a prizewinning horse. "You've got beautiful eyes, a gorgeous smile, great skin, great hair, and a great body. If you weren't my best friend, I would hate you." She always threatens to take me for a makeover. "Would it kill you to put on mascara and lipstick once in a while?"

Pat is arriving the day after Mother's Day. Two days later, she will drag me to the lunchtime bereavement group near Lewis and Clark College.

Today, both Palisades Elementary and Bellemont Elementary, where I teach, had early dismissal. Consistent with my agreement with Lucas to focus on the kids, I took Sam, Grace, and Joey out for a catch, while Lucas perfected his abs and Carol treated Mia to a mani-pedi.

So far, the problem is that Joey cannot throw a baseball. Soccer is big in Oregon but, back where I'm from, baseball is bigger. As I understand it, clichéd as it sounds, throwing a baseball is the male animal's way of having a conversation. I hope the wordless back and forth ritual will help everybody bond. "Good arm!" and "nice get" is an hour's worth of baseball talk.

Joey's first reaction to my suggestion that we play was "I'm not that kind of kid."

"Too bad," I said.

"You can't say that."

"Why not?"

"Because it's not politically correct."

"I'm not that kind of mother," I said.

"What kind of mother are you?" Joey asked.

"Play ball," I said. "That's the kind of mother I am."

Sam and Grace showed Joey basic throwing techniques. After several demonstrations, he was still stepping into his throw with the wrong foot. Maybe we could build up his confidence with batting. Or golf, because some players say it's the same swing, only sideways.

"Do you play golf?" I asked.

"I'm not a golf kind of kid."

"How about tennis?"

"I'm not a tennis kind of kid either."

"What kind of kid are you?"

"I enjoy fencing and drama."

"You're pretty good at wall climbing," Sam added, with Grace nodding.

Great. I am thinking that this is very grim and that both Carol and Lucas should spend more time with their chubby child on the playing field because one of the biggest crocks my generation was fed is "If the parents are happy, the child will be happy." I've seen a lot of physically fit parents who are very happy and their kids are pudgy and miserable. Conversely, I am (circumstantially) traumatized and miserable, but my kids are getting happier despite their circumstances.

The other crock is with regard to quality versus quantity time (and I say this both as a parent and a teacher): kids will take quantity time any time. Most kids from Happy Selfish parents will say that the one thing they always wanted, even before they could talk, was time with their parents. Which is why, for these particular parents, a global recession might not be an entirely bad thing. When parents are working too hard and doing the right thing for their physique, they are not necessarily doing the right thing for their children.

Sometimes, especially when Moms and Dads are pressed for time, I am suggesting that a great Mom may have cellulite and a good Dad is a fat dad.

The kids had started to fight. Sam called Joey a loser. Joey shouted, "I know you are, but what am I?"

A debate about mitts followed. Though Joey could not play baseball, he was extremely opinionated about what he believes to be the best equipment.

"Your Wilson's not up to par," Joey said.

"What's the matter with it?"

"You need a Mizuno."

"Why?"

"It's Japanese. They know more about baseball than we do."

"Who says so?"

"My Dad," Joey said matter-of-factly. "You need a Mizuno with the power lock Velcro band for your wrist. He read it in Consumer Reports."

"Ignore him, Sam," Grace said.

"What does your Dad think?"

"Out of bounds!" I interrupted.

Sam burst into tears.

"Our Dad's dead, you idiot!" Grace yelled.

Joey was silenced, but not for long.

He asked, "How did he die?"

I said, "Shut up, Joey."

I put my arms around Sam. He allowed me to hold him for one long, convulsive sob, then he sighed and, because he is turning ten this year, he pushed me away and wiped his eyes.

"What good is any mitt if you don't know how to catch?" Sam sniffled.

"I'm sorry, Sam," Joey said. "I didn't know."

"Well, now you do," I said quietly.

"I have an idea," Joey said.

And because Joey does not quit, we stared at him in disbelief, as if he had dropped in from one of the new Kepler planets; then he stunned us with a solution that was both judicious and very practical.

"Sam," he said, "you can punch me if you want." Joey stood arms akimbo, closed his eyes, and braced for the jab.

Sam was winding up his swing when Lucas tackled me from behind, folding his arms around my waist, and peered at the children from over my shoulder.

"Thanks for having Joey over," he said. He smiled his post-work-out smile—a smile that's stubbornly positive and oblivious to reality. "The kids are getting along great."

Sam dropped his arm and Joey's eyes popped open. After seeing the startled look on the children's faces, I unhooked Lucas's arms from my waist.

"Are you trying to date my Mom?" Grace asked. Along with Sam, Grace looked confused, as if Lucas had violated the terms of an unwritten agreement in which Lucas was primarily Grace and Sam's climbing-wall buddy and a father to Joey and Mia.

"I thought we were playing football!" Lucas smiled, deflecting Grace's question.

She held up her hot-pink mitt and matching ball.

"Baseball, Dad," Joey said.

"And you're not supposed to tackle a woman," Grace said, eyes narrowing in protest.

Half an hour later, after the kids had worked everything out with heartfelt apologies all around, Joey climbed into the back of his father's Jeep. Lucas pulled me aside, saying that he wished he could stay the night.

"We have an agreement," I said. "Our kids are going through enough. By the way, if the subject comes up, I did tell Joey to shut up."

"Why?"

"Because Joey was going on and on –"

"He does that –"

"...about Sam's crappy mitt and citing you as an expert about Japanese mitts. Sam does not have a father to deploy in the my-daddy-knows-more-than-your-daddy argument."

"I'll talk to him."

"You don't have to. Grace screamed 'Our Daddy's dead!' I'm surprised it didn't come up sooner. Kids talk about everything."

"Yes, but Joey does a lot of the talking sometimes."

"And thinking. Which is why he came up with the perfect solution."

"I'm scared to ask." He looked over at Joey, who was lost in his thoughts and sitting in the Jeep more patiently than any ten-year-old I had ever met.

"He offered to let Sam punch him."

Lucas smiled because, despite Joey's quirks—or perhaps because of them—he adores his son. "It's my fault Joey didn't know," he said. "I was worried that if I told Joey he'd ask more questions about how Sam's dad died."

"That's exactly what he did!" I laughed.

"What did you say?"

"We didn't get that far. Joey was steeling himself for

Sam's punch when you showed up."

"What do you want me to tell Joey and Mia?"

"That their father died in a gas explosion in New York City. They're too young to know the rest."

"Is that what you told Sam and Grace?"

"Yes."

Lucas called Joey out of the car. The perpetually inquisitive light in Joey's eyes had dimmed to the dull gaze of an ordinary boy about to be punished. Lucas waved Sam and Grace over.

"It's my fault Joey didn't know about your father," Lucas said, tapping his abdomen and standing much as Joey had, but with considerably more strength to endure Sam's punch. "Go for it, Sam. I interrupted your swing."

I looked at Lucas. He nodded.

Then Sam looked at me. "Your choice, buddy," I said.

I was touched and amused by Lucas's parenting choices.

Joey stepped next to his father in solidarity. "One for each of us," he smiled, once again bracing for the hit.

"Mr. Schell is a muscle man, but go easy on Joey!" Grace piped up.

At the sight of Lucas and Joey, father and son, standing side by side to make amends, Sam's eyes brimmed, then overflowed with tears. His anger had evaporated. He no longer wanted to punch anybody.

Nobody can give him his father back.

That night, I had a stormy dream. I don't know if it's because Lucas's ex-wife-to-be is a human weather system or because I am overwhelmed by today's massive feelings encased and erupting in my children's

45

small bodies and psyches. Or if it is due to my seismic excitement that East is coming West—Pat arrives in four days! Or the fact that Mother's Day is this weekend and my mother was christened Jeanne and her death coincided with Hurricane Jeanne.

I am flying Jet Blue and TRACKING JEANNE, my mother VIA LIVE SATELLITE on The Weather Channel. Damage from Jeanne – ABACO, Bahamas. Landfall by midnight.

The woman seated next to me is watching a pelvic operation on The Learning Channel. She appears fascinated. For me, it's torture: an up close and personal encounter with my mother's tumor.

Will Jeanne rival Katrina? Hurricane Jeanne, now 150 miles per hour: MANDATORY EVACUATION OF PALM BEACH. My mother's face flashes before me as the TV anchor is buffeted by gusts of wind and rain. *"Ridicule,"* she comments with a Gallic snort, as the meteorologist's mike blows off. Her face vanishes. JEANNE RACING OVER THE FLORIDA TREA-SURE COAST.

The woman seated next to me asks if I am feeling all right. I nod. I am beaming: "Jeanne is my mother."

Hurricane means Evil God of the Caribbean. With Jeanne tearing down power lines, blowing off shingles, and raising the very level of the sea, I feel the presence of my mother, my personal Fury, screaming, howling and spewing her rage, along with mine: She did not go quietly; she was not ready to go.

4

BEREAVERS I

Finally, after years, months, weeks of counting down and three days after receiving a cerulean clay dog from Sam and one illuminated poem from Grace on Mother's Day, Pat is here and about to pick me up.

I am getting a pedicure.

Pedicures count as one way I have gone native. Out East, I know the secret world of sturdy New England girls. At the gym, they pull off their pants and shoes revealing legs with entire Brillo jungles, stiff enough to scrub a burnt test tube clear. Their feet are so unnaturally white, waxen and fungal, they're a case study in anaerobic forms of life. I have seen toes long enough to strum a classical guitar.

I've gone native in a way that improves my personal hygiene. So far, I've had two pedicures. The first was a few days after my mother was diagnosed with cancer. I walked in, sat in the spa chair, and stared at the sapphire water swirling around my toes.

"My name is Mimi. Yours?"

I looked up. "Juliette."

"Pretty name," she smiled. "Color?"

I got up, selected cranberry, and sat back down in the spa chair, which Mimi turned into a massage chair by punching buttons on its remote. Mimi took the nail polish and placed it on her tray.

"Nice color."

Mimi is thirtysomething and petite with shiny black hair clipped back with a gold and pink floral hair claw. When she speaks English, she has a slight Vietnamese accent. Color is C*owah*. Cancer is Can*sah*. Mother is Moth*ah*.

"Thank you."

"How you?"

"Mom sick," I said.

"Sad."

"Dad sick" I said.

"Oh. Too sad."

"Everybody dying," I said, getting into the swing of her present tense because, after all, that's all there is.

"My mama died," she said.

"I'm very sorry," I said.

"Cancer," she said. "Cancer bad."

"Cancer *very* bad."

Mimi sensed all the pulsating leather settings unsettling me. She reached over and punched the off button on the massage chair.

"Thank you," I said.

What followed was 15 minutes of pure silence. But it was hardly indifferent. Mimi worked hard, trimming carefully, massaging my calves, applying cream and polish.

After she had put on the clear top coat, she patted my shin to signal she was done and started cleaning up.

Today, I walked into the same nail salon. The owner pointed to the next available chair with a woman I did not know. "Mimi from Saigon," I said.

I caught her eye. Mimi rushed over with a big smile. "Mother?"

"Mother dead," I said. Then I started to cry.

All the women, along with Tony, the owner of the shop, started scurrying around, ushering me to a seat. "Massage chair free," Tony cried in a nervous whine. He gathered their best magazines. Before long, I had a two-foot stack of *Real Simple, Star*, and *InStyle*. Tony ran over with an issue of *People*. "New one!" he smiled.

I thanked Tony and poured out my whole story to Mimi. I told her about my mother, the hospital, the HIPPA regulations, the medication that came or did not come in the mail, my father's lung cancer, the search for caregivers, the funeral, the burial, and my daughter's memorial rocks.

Mimi nodded in sympathy and looked increasingly serious. With my last revelation, she looked up and said, "I have a daughter too."

Which made me think of my so-called friend Amy, who phoned from the Galapagos to apologize for missing my mother's funeral. In the same breath, she suggested that I join "one of those bereavement groups." Off of her desk, onto Mimi's instrument tray.

"One month. Come back." Mimi smiled. "We talk again."

"Absolutely." I said. "We talk again."

As I drive through the leafy encampment known as Tryon Creek State Park, Pat tells me that her working hypothesis is that suffering and loss are treated differently on the West Coast. "If that's the case," she says, "I might write an article."

This news heartens me. Sometime after Mr. Sanders' 11th Grade writing workshop, and sometime before Pat got her degree in flower arranging at the Bronx Botanical Gardens, Pat was a magnificent writer. She wrote a biography of Marlene Dietrich, claiming that it was authorized and that she had interviewed her. The book was a bestseller until one of Dietrich's apostles called in on national television and insisted that Dietrich had never heard of Pat. The man claimed that *he* would know because *he* had kept Marlene's schedule, along with detailed inventories of her wigs and her Tupperware collection.

Along with the lawyer who failed to give Pat's book a proper legal read, two hundred thousand books were ritualistically slaughtered in the publishing house's *abattoir*. Pat never wrote another word.

The road from our Lake Oswego suburb to the Nature Center is solid green. Rarely do the leaves part. When they do, misty steel patches of sky appear like fragments in a kaleidoscope. It's the kind of day that drove my father's ancestors in County Mayo to drink whiskey. It's the kind of day that makes my hands itch for a buzz saw. God forbid anyone in Oregon should yell, *Timber!*

For most of the ride, Pat marvels at how green Oregon is. "So much moss and mud!"

The moss covers lawns, forests, and roofs in a manner so thick they look upholstered. In some houses, even fancy ones, you half-expect a gnome to emerge.

I cannot find the Nature Center, but it found us. I drove up what turned out to be the building's wheelchair ramp and dropped off Pat, one foot shy of the glass door. I waved to the park attendant inside. She smiled back. As I shifted the car into reverse, she made a frantic run for the sapling I was heading toward and hurled herself in front to protect it.

Inside, we are surrounded by snake moltings, birds' nests, fox pelts, bug samples, seed boxes, and more moss. I don't think I had ever seen so much moss until I moved to Oregon. Moss on trees, moss on houses, not quite on humans, but almost. From October to May, Oregon is a terrarium in which even the locals take on an olive cast. They're so used to rain or drizzle and a sky ranging in shades from silver to nickel, that they don't even bother with umbrellas. The rare and occasional "sunbreak" (as they are referred to on local weather reports) restores the locals' hue to flesh tone.

The bereavers straggle in, talking quietly as they drag their folding chairs to form a circle. Pat chats with a few of them and announces in her deep, phone-sex voice: "I find this setting SO therapeutic." All heads turn in her direction; they cannot take their eyes off Pat.

The group leader is Brenda. She is here because her six-year-old was hit by a school bus as she watched from the curb. Brenda is forty and is unable to have another child. She stands twice the height of her stacking chair. Her skin is pale. Her pale blue eyes hide like small marbles behind her silver, wire-framed glasses. Her wavy, fine hair is the color of ash. Everything about Brenda is pale and gentle. If she were a cuisine, she would probably be Scandinavian—muted colors, no flare or spice, but gentle and reliable. This is the sort of person I feel comfortable with for this particular job description.

We go around the room to introduce ourselves. Some people are matter of fact as to why they attend; others are not ready to talk. Ann is here because her son hit a tree in a snowboarding accident. Mike's here because his daughter overdosed on painkillers. Jim's here because his lover committed suicide. Samantha's here because her husband was gunned down in Iraq, and Cheryl's here because her husband died of kidney failure.

I do not tell them why I am here, and Brenda says that I do not have to. Pat's the talker. Let her share. Instead, a woman with a small, oval face raised her hand.

"My name is Macy," she said. "I've never attended a bereavement group, and this is not a typical death, so I'm timid about sharing."

"Don't be," Brenda said. "This is not a typical group."

Macy looks Goth: a black pixie haircut, enormous eyes, a thin and delicate frame, and three visible tattoos—a gargoyle, Medusa, and a baby.

"It all started when a stranger called me," she began. "The stranger said, 'I'm sorry to have to tell you this, but I've just received word that Hugh Michael is dead.'"

"Hugh Michael was his name?" Brenda jotted that down on her roster.

"Yes."

"Sorry to interrupt. Please continue."

"The caller said, 'Hugh Michael died in a car crash near Monaco. Your name was in his wallet.' I asked the woman who she was in relation to Hugh. 'His ex-wife', she said. I told her I was sorry. 'Yes, it's sad,' she said. 'We were on good terms. Still the best of friends.'"

Pat and I sat, sipping our Zen tea, swallowing every word. Since Macy had told Pat that she was happily married to a big, burly computer software programmer named Jesse, we were doubly curious about Hugh Michael.

"Who's Hugh Michael?" Pat asked.

Brenda flashed Pat a kind but firm look that said *I'll lead this group, thank you very much.* "I'm going to ask all of you to reserve your comments," she added.

Macy didn't seem to notice the exchange. "I'm very nervous," she said. "I met him once."

Brenda asked Macy why the death of someone she'd met once had brought her to the group.

Good question. This might sound petty, especially when the subject is grief, but loss can get competitive. I cannot speak for Brenda, but I can tell you flat out that if I had seen one of my children hit and killed by a school bus, I would wonder if Macy's grief weighed as much as mine. I cannot imagine anyone's grief being worse than Brenda's. Bad enough that your child is hit by the friendly yellow school bus. Bad enough that you love and trust the driver and buy him presents at every opportunity in order that he not retire from the most miserable job on the planet (second to being a subway booth clerk at the Times Square Eighth Avenue Line). Bad enough that your child dies from being hit by the friendly, yellow school bus with the driver you (and your child's teacher!) have come to love and trust. Worst of all: That you SEE your child killed by someone you have come to love and trust and through no fault of his own–other than momentary inattentiveness, of which any parent is guilty, but for which the bus driver will pay the price for the rest of his life and will never sleep soundly again. From bad to worse to unbearable to unendurable.

Brenda listens sympathetically to Macy and presumably to all of us. Who listens to Brenda? Someone must. Someone pulled her through, perhaps more than one. Why else would she do this? How else could she sit there and listen to any of us? With the exception of Nick, the deaths of my Grandmother and my parents were, at the very least, in the natural order of things. I think that most of us who are suffering are keen on getting the answer to Brenda's question: Why is Macy here?

After a few minutes of silence, Macy said, "I am haunted by the fact that someone I had forgotten considered me so memorable."

I am haunted by the fact that someone I had forgotten considered me so memorable.

With this, she introduced a stunningly metaphysical quality to the bereavement group.

Jim gasped. It was very slight but a gasp, nonetheless.

Pat whipped out her reporter's notebook and started taking notes, beginning with her neat, huge 18 point Catholic cursive: *"I am haunted by the fact that someone I had forgotten considered me so memorable."*

Pat's foot was tapping like crazy. I had seen her like this once before, when she was ghost-writing a book for Anita Hill during the Clarence Thomas hearings. Pat's foot went metronome when Anita mentioned pubic hair on the Coke can.

"What are you doing?" Brenda asked Pat.

"Taking notes."

"No notes," Brenda said, trying to conceal her irritation. "Anything said in the group stays in the group."

"Everything happens for a reason," Ann pronounced with a serenity that was mostly evangelical.

Brenda glanced at the clock and thanked Macy for sharing her story, then she fixed her eyes on Pat. "Would you like to share, Pat?"

"No. Thank you. I'd rather listen for now." She was fidgeting in her chair. "But my friend, Juliette, here. Juliette lost her…"

Brenda cut her off, turning to me. "Do you wish to share, Juliette?" she asked.

"No, thank you. I'm not prepared," I said.

More than unprepared, the strangest thing had just occurred. Listening to Macy's story about Hugh Michael triggered another memory of Michael Rolland. I came to the group with a set number of people I intended to mourn, but my heart was ripped open further to include a man I had loved and lost decades ago. I was so distracted by his resurgent presence that I pictured him sitting in the corner of the Nature Center waiting for me—patient, kind, breathtakingly beautiful, and manly as any rugby-playing Black Celt has ever been. I was reliving the anguish I felt on the day we took the Tube to Heathrow. "Leaving you might be the worst mistake I'll ever make," I said.

I stood up to rush over and throw my arms around him when I felt a hand jerking mine. "Sit down!" Pat rasped, pulling me back to my chair. "Read them something from your journal," she said, jogging me out of my reverie.

Brenda reminded us that letters, poems, memoir entries, dream journals—anything that helps us express our feelings toward those we have lost—can be a powerful therapeutic tool. Cheryl raised her hand to say she had started writing a blog for kidney donors. Pat tried to raise mine, again, but I gripped the bottom of my chair so firmly that my nail broke when it jabbed a hardened wad of bubble gum.

"I'd like to hear something from Juliette and Cheryl when you are ready," Brenda said.

"Me too," Samantha said. Mike and Ann nodded in agreement.

As we were leaving, Ann invited our bereavement group to a spa party benefitting her son Jake's school. Before I could check for any conflict in my calendar, Pat said, "We'll be there."

On the way back to Lake Oswego, I reminded Pat that Grace had a soccer game. She lit up a cigarette and I told her to snuff it out.

"Will they allow me to smoke at Gracie's soccer game? It's *outside*."

"That's up to the Oregonians. They take pride in their air quality."

"What did you think of the group?" she asked.

"I love Brenda and I liked the people."

"Me too. I was thinking that Macy might be a good friend for you. She's a librarian."

"I was completely undone by her Hugh Michael story."

"You still are."

"What do you mean?"

"You just drove through a red light."

"SHIT!"

"Is that why you stood up before we adjourned?"

"For some reason, Macy's story brought Michael Rolland raging back."

"Oh!" She almost coughed out her cigarette. "What a tender, brilliant gorgeous man!"

"You're the only person who met him," I said.

"He was well worth the trip to London. When he blinked his long black lashes and gazed at me with those gorgeous emerald eyes, telling me he loved you 'something fierce' with that faint Irish lilt of his, I just melted."

Macy's story had drilled some kind of portal in my mind and the details were flooding through. A beach, a museum, a park, a heath, a piggyback ride down the road leading to Ely Cathedral (his favorite). We could not keep our hands off each other.

"God, how I loved him," I said.

"Do you regret not staying?"

"I regret going to the bereavement group if it's going to dredge up losses from the past," I said, blinking back tears. "Don't make me sad," I added, snapping back to the practical world of Grace's soccer practice. "I had to go back for graduate school, and you know the rest."

"He kept promising he'd move to the States."

"And I traveled back and forth for two and a half agonizing years."

Pat must have sensed my mood decaying as predictably as the brick of peat Michael had sent to the States from County Mayo as a Christmas gift for the Irish relatives on my father's side of the family.

"What about the guy with the orange hair who was your antidote to Michael? He was fun."

"He *was* fun," I laughed. "But nothing works when you're fused to someone, mind, body, and soul. And I'll thank you *not* to review my inventory of former flames."

"Why not? You're single."

"So are *you*! What's going on with Bill?"

"I don't know."

"What does that mean?"

"It means we're not doing so well."

Given the demands of teaching, motherhood, the bereavement group—along with the 3000 miles and three time zones between us—I realized that Pat and I never had enough time catch up on the essential details best friends share.

"For starters, I promised him I'd give up smoking."

"I'm all for that!"

"His consulting business is taking off so he's constantly out of town," Pat said. She lit another cigarette and reminded me to slow down so I didn't run another red light. "We never see each other, and I never know where he is."

"He's welcome to visit," I offered.

"Really?"

"Of course." Pat helps me feel at home in Oregon. She can stay as long as she likes, though I did need to know *approximately* how many weeks. "How long are you staying?"

"I just got here!"

"I know. It's just that Management needs to honor all reservations. If the grandparents and Bill visit, I'll need to shuffle things around. What kind of consultant is he?"

"Security consultant."

"What does that mean?"

"It means he's constantly traveling and going to meetings with private and public clients."

"Did Macy tell you where she worked?" I turned into the parking lot closest to the field, determined to finish one adult conversation with my best friend.

"Multnomah County is what she told me. What does Multnomah mean?"

"They're a tribe of Chinookan people who lived in the Portland area until the 19th century. They are part of the Penutian family."

"This American Indian stuff is *fascinating*." Pat feigned interest in order to take an exceptionally long drag on her cigarette.

"You should read up on the Wampanoag back East." Lucas had given me a book about King Philip's War. "I love teaching our fourth-grade Native American curriculum, but my little Oregonians hate it when they get stuck with the East coast tribes."

"I like Macy," Pat resumed, "but I thought Brenda was *very* tough on me."

"Oh come on, Pat! You *know* you can't take notes!"

I pulled into a parking spot and grabbed two rain ponchos from the back seat.

"I couldn't help it," she said. "You have to admit this is a potentially *fabulous* story."

I pointed to her cigarette. She took another two furtive puffs and crushed the butt under her Italian boot. I handed her a poncho.

"No way I'm wearing that thing," she said.

I decided to use Pat's reservations about Brenda to my advantage.

"So we won't be going back next Wednesday, right?"

"Wrong. Same time next week."

"We talk again," as Mimi would say.

5

SNAKES IN THE GRASS

The wild part of the Wild West is that Grace spotted a rattlesnake where her team, the Kixie Chicks, play soccer. The not-so-wild, 21st century, politically correct part is that no one's allowed to kill it.

One of the coaches called a policeman, who arrived within minutes.

"Get rid of it," I said.

I did not want any details. I was sure they had statutes dealing with serpentine euthanasia. I just wanted the rattler off the field where, let's face it, a few crazy fangings and it's curtains for the third-grade tournament.

"It's a protected animal," the officer said.

"You're joking," I said.

"No, ma'am"

"Kill it," Pat demanded.

"Kill it," another father echoed. But he was from California, so he was perceived with greater suspicion than either the reptile or an Easterner.

I called Lucas, thinking he might display some date-worthy snake-wrangling mojo.

"Is he coming?" Pat asked.

"He's on his way," I said.

"I'm stressed. I need a ciggie." Pat lit her Salem Light and followed another parent across the street into the school construction site, where they collared a landscaper.

I don't know what arrangements they made with him, but I did see Pat offer him a cigarette. All I know is that after I'd evacuated eight screaming Kixie Chicks from the field, the landscaper looked the snake in the eye and had second thoughts.

"Can't do it," he said. "Sorry."

"Why not?"

"It's a living thing."

"So are we!" Pat cried. "What a pussy," she muttered.

"What did you call me!?"

She took a long drag on her cigarette and said, very calmly, "I don't know how to say it in Oregonian."

I looked at my roster and after a moment's hesitation called Lucas again. His daughter had a game right after ours and he was coaching.

"What about *him*?" Pat said, when, fifteen minutes later, she saw a man approach. "Nice legs. Nice package."

"That's Lucas," I said.

He hurried towards me with Mia. His mesh bag bulged with glossy, neon-green soccer balls and neon-orange cones.

"Anyone call for a snake-whisperer?" Lucas kissed me too slowly on each cheek. Pats eyes widened with a you-see, you-never-know expression and she smiled with approval.

"Charm it or kill it," I said quietly. I did not want to upset Mia and, at the risk of avoiding the incident we'd had with Sam and Joey, I asked Lucas if he had told Mia about Grace's father.

"Yes," he said. "But Grace had already told her."

"Figures!" I laughed at Grace's pluck and honesty. I was profoundly relieved that she was confiding in her friend.

"Lucas, this is my best friend, Pat, who is visiting from New York," I said.

"Welcome," he said, greeting her with a solid handshake. "Juliette talks about you all the time."

"Well, she talks about *you* all the time too!" Pat said, and I wanted to kill her.

"I'm crazy about her," he said, wrapping his arm around my shoulder and giving it a squeeze. "Can you watch Mia for me while I go snake hunting?"

"Sure."

"I'll come with you," Pat said.

"Daddy, she's *smoking*," Mia said. Her face tilted up like a sunflower—open, honest, and appealing.

"Do you mind putting that out?" he asked.

"Absolutely not," Pat smiled.

"I don't want to give her mom any more ammo," he whispered to Pat. "We're separated."

Half an hour later, the rattler disappeared and nobody is supposed to talk about it. If we do, it's likely that one of the landscapers will end up tending shrubs in a prison yard.

I asked the City of Lake Oswego to fax me information in the event of a future snake encounter or, worse still, a snake attack. They told me that what we had seen was not possible. According to their Natural Resource Coordinator, "Rattlesnakes have been extirpated from the Willamette valley." Later, after viewing another snake, which appeared in my neighbor's garden the following week, we were told what we should have done:

1) Back slowly away from the snake

2) Do not attempt to handle the snake

3) Do not attempt to kill the snake

4) Generously flag off the area where they were found

5) Hang warning signs

6) Notify the police at 503-635-0000 and/or the Natural Resource Coordinator at 503-697-0000.

Then, they issued this flyer:

> Rattlesnakes can be easily identified by their broad flat diamond-shaped head, presence of rattles on the tail (not always on very small ones), vertical pupils in eyes, diamond shapes on a broad body, and generally greenish to tan coloring. They can make a rattling sound with their tail. Adult snakes are 30-40 inches. They will rarely strike at a human unless harassed. Most injuries are the result of someone attempting to handle them. If a rattlesnake bites you, remain

calm and seek medical assistance immediately.
Call 911.

Blah, blah, blah.

After the game, Pat and I went for a walk in the neighborhood. Despite Grace's last-minute goal, securing a victory for the Kixie Chicks, Pat was still jittery after the rattlesnake incident. She is an animal lover to the core. I felt we had no other choice, but Pat thought we had behaved no better than children who, as the self-appointed gods of their micro-world, casually crush ladybugs or spiders. Inside, we are shouting, STOP THE GENOCIDE. To the children, we say, "Leave it alone. It's not bothering you."

Sam and Grace are tagging along. Around the corner from the school, we lift them above the fence so they can pet Dolly the llama on our neighbor's farm. Grace brings the pack of carrots from her lunch and feeds the horse in the meadow near our rental house. Sam throws the tennis ball for our neighbor's terrier, Jackie, who stops to christen a new sign in the construction zone on the far side of the school playground. Do Not Enter Without Project Arborist Approval.

"Can you imagine a sign like that being posted in Larchmont?" I asked Pat.

We pass by a barn, cut through a local vineyard, and step onto a dirt trail that climbs into Cook Butte Park. Pat marvels at Oregon's natural beauty. "It's so green, so unspoiled. That red barn looks like it belongs in New

England and you're fifteen minutes away from Portland."

Jackie starts barking frantically and takes off after a squirrel. She leaps, digs, climbs, and jumps as if she'd have a shot at scaling Oregon's Phalanx, the world's tallest ponderosa pine measuring 268 feet.

"Still," Pat says, "it must have been tough moving here. I mean, *where are all the people!?*"

Pat is very New York. If the population density is under ten people per square foot, she feels the oncoming panic of solitude.

"That wasn't the tough part."

"What was?"

"We are not from here. They do not know us."

"You've only been here two years."

"I'd hoped people would be more welcoming. Especially when we first arrived. Sam was not the boy who drew Spiderman with a Sharpie on school bus seats, but they *thought* he was. Grace was not the girl who stuck bubble gum under the tables in the library, but they *thought* she was. Lucas is not the Level 3 Sex Offender the Portland Police have been scouring the forest for, but my neighbor called the police the first time he knocked on my door."

"How many times has he knocked on your door?" Pat laughed that rich, naughty laugh of hers and turned to the kids. "Do you like Lucas?" she asked.

Sam and Gracie groaned.

"Why are you moaning, children?" Pat asked cheerfully.

"Mom is spending too much time with Lucas," Grace said.

"His son's a spaz," Sam said.

"Sports-challenged," I corrected.

"No. Grace is sports-challenged. Joey's a total spaz."

"MOM! You heard him!" She kicked her brother in the shin.

"MOM! You SAW that!"

Grace started imitating Lucas. She pumped up her toothpick arms. "Lucas is a muscle man," she said with a thick, Slavic accent.

When she kissed her puny bicep, I said, "Let's change the subject."

"Yeah, let's talk about broccoli," Sam said. "Mom's favorite subject. Pat, do you have any idea how much broccoli Mom makes us eat!?"

"How much?"

"Since we moved here, at *least* twice a week," Grace said.

"Broccoli contains—"

"Antioxidants!" Sam and Grace shouted in droll monotone.

"Grandma and Grandpa ate broccoli all the time," Sam said. "They both died of cancer." He is angry. He loved them. "That's all they ate," he said. "Broccoli, broccoli, broccoli. Dead, dead, dead." His eyes well up and I cannot bear it. "I miss them," Sam said. "They were so much fun."

Pat put her arms around Sam. "They were fun, Sam. You're lucky. My grandparents bored the shit out of me."

The kids are smiling, but I say, "Watch your mouth, Pat."

"Oh, come on, Juliette. Sam's going to be ten next

month and Gracie will be nine in September. They're old enough."

"Yeah, Mom," Sam insisted. "We can say shit."

Pat tripped over Jackie and fell into what looked like an ordinary patch of mud, but when she tried to step out, her favorite Italian boots got sucked down as an offering to the mud God, who is really trafficking in clay. Jackie jumped in to save Pat and emerged looking like a terrier dipped in chocolate. Pat walked home in bare feet with a mud line around her hips.

"Very funny," she snarled, when it became impossible to disguise our amusement.

As we neared the horse meadow, Lily, our seven-year-old neighbor, started pointing at Pat. Her mother, Mrs. Jenny Anderson, whispered something in Lily's ear, took her by the hand, and led her inside.

"Not very friendly," Pat said.

"Jackie is!" Grace said. "She's the Anderson's dog."

"Even Jackie would rather live with us," Sam said. "We're at war."

"What happened?" Pat asked.

"Lily was mean to Grace."

"I thought you hated Gracie."

"I do, but she's my sister."

Sam is at war with Lily's family because racial profiling is alive and well in the dark recesses of their miserable marriage and newly renovated kitchen. He punched Lily during our first summer here when her first neighborly words to Grace were, "I don't want to play with you. You have brown hair and brown skin."

The parents denied that their midget white

supremacist had said anything of the kind. "We spoke with Lily. She would never say such a thing!"

Our mixed heritage has not helped Sam, who, like many nine-year-old boys, is perfectly capable of making an alienating impression in his own right.

As Lily walked away, Sam yelled, "Don't worry, Lily. Pat's not brown. It's just mud."

"Maybe they just wanted their dog back," Pat said.

"I don't think that helped, Samuel," I said firmly. "I teach in the public schools here. We are members of the community."

"No we're *not!*" His eyes welled up. "I miss Dad. He would punch everybody in the face."

I was incapable of responding. Then Grace's innocent question made it worse.

"Mom, do you miss Daddy?"

I was paralyzed.

"Of *course* she does!" Pat said. "Sam, Grace. Come help me wash Jackie. She looks like a Raisinet!"

That evening, while Pat was inviting Bill to come to Oregon, I needed to communicate with my family.

Letter to the Afterlife

Dearest Mom, Dad, and Grandmere,

On our walk, today, Sam and Grace ("Mom, do you miss Daddy?") said perfectly normal things which stirred up a seismic rage I had no idea I possessed. Thanks to Pat, who put them to work washing our neighbor's dog, I was able to suppress my reflexive urge to say something atrocious, loathsome, but entirely true about their father. The time he was a no-show in the ER after Sam's first-grade playdate shot him one inch from his eye with a BB gun. Another no-show in the ER when Grace swallowed "hot-pink candies" that turned out to be Benadryl. One day later, I was subpoenaed in my classroom, again, only to learn that Nick's no-shows to the ER were deliberate.

"Bad parenting." Mine, his lawyer argued. Nick refused all medical bills (the parent who takes the child to the ER is required to sign a paper accepting all financial responsibility) and the judge awarded Nick full custody on weekdays.

This is too much information but, now that you're gone, I have nobody other than Pat to talk to about this muck. Actually, I have to be careful about telling Pat everything because she would take out a contract on Nick if he were not already dead.

On the bright side, *dwelling* on Sam's remark ironically ended up helping me. "I miss Dad. He would punch everybody in the face" triggered fond memories of your outrageously negative parental motivational techniques.

In fairness to all three of you, the tactics actually worked!

Grandmere,

You always put a *THAT'S WHY* causal spin on things.

You let the dog run out and *THAT'S WHY* he was run over!

You didn't put your shoes on and *THAT'S WHY* you stepped on a nail!

You ate too much cake and *THAT'S WHY* you have the stomach flu!

You talked back to your mother and *THAT'S WHY* she's in the hospital!

You got a bad report card and *THAT'S WHY* your parents are considering a divorce.

Mom,

You refined your mother's Old School Technique. It always started with: I knew a little girl who (*Je connaissais une petite fille qui......*)

I knew a little girl who always slammed doors.
I knew a little girl who ate too many candies.
I knew a little girl who played doctor with a little boy.
I knew a little girl who lied about her report card.

I knew a little girl who did not look both ways when she crossed the street.

"And what happened to the little girl?" I would ask.

In the following order: The Doorslammer lost three fingers. Sweet Tooth's permanent teeth came in rotten. Girl who Played Doctor had a baby at 12. Liar liar pants-on-fire went to jail. And Girl Who Only Looked One Way was squashed like a bug.

I remember saying, "There can't be *that* many dead children."

Dad,

I am renting a house in Oregon and regret selling our family home back east. From here, it's impossible to handle lawn work, frozen pipes, gutters, storm windows, puff back from the furnace, and the other small epics of home ownership.

Love,
Juliette

When I feel out of sorts during the day, I invariably find myself at night walking through my childhood home. Outside, I wait for the school bus. I can tell you the texture of the dirt and pebbles under the curb, and the extent to which the toes on my Buster Browns were scuffed, depending on the season. I can hear Mrs. Dunn's old muffler as she approaches. I can see Stuart Freedman throwing *The Reporter Dispatch* and missing his mark.

I trace geographies of places that feel like home. Things are so detailed that I walk by every varnished oak door in my elementary school. I need to be certain that Miss Nickerson, Mrs. Robinson, Mrs. Lowe, Miss Howes, Mrs. Brailey, and Miss MacMahon are still there, and that Mrs. O'Brien is teaching chorus.

I should keep a list of all the things my parents used to say because, nowadays, their words arrive from out of nowhere, washing over me like warm waves of affection; their retreat leaves me sad, exposed, and lonely. Truisms like "Nothing intelligent is said after ten o'clock at night" were delivered like the crack of a whip by my mother, with her French accent and dung-sniffing expressions. At the time, her remark justified keeping me home while girls like Pat were out playing Spin the Bottle or Truth or Dare.

Now that my parents and the other guardians of these small histories have died, I am compelled to set things down before I forget them altogether, and before things won't be the way they were. My children ask me where I'm from. I tell them about my childhood home, but the home in my dreams feels like home only because it is still inhabited by those I love. I wonder if it would feel the same empty; or would it resemble a body, once its soul had, so to speak, left the building.

One thing I have learned. One thing I will I never do. I will never again pay my respects to a dead loved one who has been gone for more than five minutes. Years ago, I went to see my uncle after he died. His body faced me as I walked into his bedroom. His liver had failed. He was yellow as a lemon. My aunt had not closed one of his eyes. It stared out like a blue marble. His soul had left the building.

6

SECURITY BREACH

I had just extracted myself from another one of Lucas's gentle tackles during a round of touch football when I noticed a smile on Sam's face. His smile grew like one of those slow smiles you see on a cowboy's face in a Western, when the partner he thought long dead walks into Cheyenne towards him.

The partner was Pat's boyfriend, Bill. He had grabbed a football from our garage and was running over to introduce himself when Grace shouted, "MOM! Look! It's the man from the airport who saved Kaya!"

I was brought up properly and, under normal circumstances, am quite polite and efficient about introducing people. But REWIND.

Pat had just pulled into our driveway with Bill from the Los Angeles Airport. She had picked him up at the Portland airport. "Surprise!" she said.

Allow me to convey my complete shock, disbelief, and mortification that Pat's college boyfriend is none other than my Mr. LAX Airport Security Encounter.

This man is staying at my house, which means that, suddenly, Bill Cunningham, not Bob Cummings, is staying at my house.

I was so flustered that Bill—not Bob, as I had heard at the airport—Cunningham took it upon himself to introduce himself to Lucas and his children. Then Lucas re-introduced himself to Pat, who was stepping from leaf to leaf to avoid getting mud on her replacement Italian boots.

"Nice to see you again, Lucas," Pat said. "My, my," she said, scanning his torso, "you *have* been working out!" Off went her naughty laugh.

"Thanks. That's why…" he looked around to make sure the children were out of range. "That's why Juliette doesn't want to date me."

"Why not?"

"She thinks that men who work out are stupid."

"Shame on you!" Pat said, eyeing Lucas's Oregon State sweatshirt and giving me a scolding look. She's such a good actress that I could not tell if she meant it. This is the same Pat who told me to dump Lucas *unless* I was having bodice-ripping, kitchen-counter sex with him every other night.

Pat kept trying to introduce me to Bill. I stepped forward and got it over with. "I'm Juliette," I said. This time he reached out to grab my hand. "Nice to see you," he said. I wanted to evaporate.

"Lucas is always reading on the treadmill," I said. "But he's right about my stereotype."

"Let me guess," Bill said. "*The Great Gatsby*?"

"No," Lucas said.

"*The Power of Now*?"

76

"Why did you pick *those* two books!?" I could not help asking, given that one night I'd gone on Match.com (*because it's okay to look*) and, sure enough, under Favorite Books, many of the self-described "Educated" men picked *Gatsby* and the "Spiritual" men chose *The Power of Now.*

"Just a hunch," Bill said.

"Wrong again," Lucas said. "It's okay," he said with Lucasian confidence. "That's the kind of negative attitude that blocks Juliette's potential."

"East Coast negativity," Bill said. "We *thrive* on it."

"You're from Texas!" Pat laughed.

"I can be your personal trainer too," Lucas offered. "You'll be a lot healthier *and* your mental attitude will improve."

"Juliette told me you were an environmental lawyer," Pat said.

"I am. And I can help you quit smoking."

"*Promise?*" Bill said.

"I do."

Bill tossed the football to Lucas. "Play ball, Oregon State," he said, calling over the kids.

"I'm Grace."

"Claire's," he said. "I remember."

"I'm Sam."

"Spidey," he said, "I remember."

"I'm Joey."

"Nice to meet you."

"I'm Mia."

"Hi, Mia. Do you like Claire's as much as Grace?"

"YES!"

One stolen glance revealed a man who looked even

better than he had at LAX. In natural light, I guessed him to be about forty-four years old. He looked about five-foot eleven or so, with a solid build, beautiful, strong hands, and the kind of square-jawed handsome face I used to see on my father's Draw-Me matchbook covers. He spoke to Lucas in that spitfire, confident manner I often marvel at in Preston Sturges movies (Lewis and Clark College has been offering a black-and-white movie classics festival on Wednesdays, which is one reason the Bereavement Group is not my first choice on our district's early dismissal day). He bore no trace of a Texas accent, just its endearing, relaxed cadence.

"Pat," Bill said, "Juliette and I have met."

"How!?"

Lucas threw a lazy spiral back to Bill. Bill fired back a bullet.

Lucas groaned and doubled over. Joey ran over. "Are you okay, Dad?"

"Juliette made a suggestion to Airport Security at LAX," Bill said. "It was brilliant."

"You're kidding. Right?" Pat turned to me.

"My suggestion was hardly brilliant," I said. "If anything, it was inappropriate and, again, Bob, I mean Bill, I apologize."

"Joey, your dad's fine," Bill said. "Take the ball and throw it to Sam."

"What on earth did you suggest?" Pat asked me.

Joey threw the ball two yards short, but everyone said *good effort*! because it was a minor miracle to see Joey's ball in flight. Sam picked up the ball and threw it to Bill.

"You really know how to play!" Sam possessed the eager smile of a lesser player on a winning team.

"What exactly did Juliette *say* at the airport?" Pat asked Bill. "And what were you doing at LAX!?"

"Gracie, run out for a pass," Bill said.

"I can't."

"There's that negativity again," Lucas smiled. "Straight from her mother."

"Well then I *can't* and *won't* take you to Claire's," Bill said, with sing-songy petulance.

Grace was so charmed that she fell silent.

Bill faced Pat and, to my horror, told her about the airport mammograms. "Best suggestion I've had all year." He threw the ball to Grace and she ran as if her life depended on it. She stretched her arms like rubber bands, way beyond their natural elasticity, and caught Bill's pass. I had never seen her so focused. This was past the point of charmed and well into schoolgirl crush territory.

"Great get, Grace!" Bill shouted.

"Airport mammograms!?" Pat's eyes widened. "I thought I had problems," she said. "You're lucky it was Bill. Did you *know* it was Bill?"

"*How would I know!?*" I raised my voice, perhaps a bit too defensively.

"Bill, did you know she was *my* Juliette?"

"I do now."

"Of all the checkpoints, in all the airports, in all the world, Juliette walks into Bill's," Lucas said, hijacking the romance of *Casablanca* to claim me with a kiss on the cheek. "Pass the ball to Joey," he ordered Grace. He was tired of letting Bill quarterback.

"I don't run," Joey said.

Bill started chasing Joey.

"I'm not a running kind of kid," he panted and laughed in spite of himself.

"Then you're not a kid," Bill said. He turned to Lucas. "This is the kind of negative attitude that blocks Joey's potential." He smiled his impossibly winning smile.

Lucas was only mildly amused. Obviously *I need to resolve my own issues with Bill*, but sometimes it takes a stranger to reveal hypocrisy. Lucas has to coach his own kid in mainstream sports because unless Joey makes the Olympic team, fencing is a niche sport. Later on, Joey will have plenty of time to do the Pacific Northwest Marginal thing. Later on, he can drive a Volkswagen bus to jousting fairs all over Oregon. But first, let's aim for the mainstream because, in Oregon, the mild-to-extreme margin ranges from No Sales Tax fanatics, to Libertarians, to sociopaths who live in cabins, to thrill seekers who desecrate Oregon's spectacular dunes by driving ATVs with pink plastic testicles dangling over their hitches. By all means, *Keep Portland Weird.*

Bill threw the ball to Joey one last time. Joey tried so hard to keep his eye on the ball that you had to love this boy, making such an enormous effort. Joey caught the ball, then threw it to Grace, who threw it to me, who threw it to Pat, who threw it to Lucas.

"Hey! What about me?" Sam yelled.

Lucas gunned the ball to Sam. He doubled over, the wind knocked out of him.

"Are you okay, Sam?" Lucas asked.

Bill went over to Sam and took the ball out of his chicken-wing clutch. "Amazing catch," he said, helping him up.

Sam nodded, still a bit dazed.

"Go out for a pass, Lucas," Bill said. "This one's got your name on it." Bill fired a pass that would have burned a hole in the belly of a wide receiver from Notre Dame.

Lucas caught it with an involuntary and barely audible grunt, as if to insist it was a catch *like any other*.

Sam trudged over to Lucas. "Are you okay?" he asked.

Bill offered Lucas his hand in a sportsmanlike manner, pulling him to his feet, then walked over to Pat and put his arm around her shoulder.

"Let the games begin," she drawled, confused by the excessive hormonal build-up in the course of what started out as a friendly catch between Bill and Lucas. "And next time you're at the airport, return my damn text!" she said, smacking Bill soundly on his rear.

7

TRACKING JEANNE (BEREAVERS II)

I hate doing my taxes. All the receipts are tangible reminders of medical emergencies, movies long forgotten, abandoned toys, momentary enthusiasms, and funerals.

On thc back of my boarding passes and travel receipts to Portland, I found these jottings. I did not want to be alone with them, so I brought them to our second bereavement meeting.

Mom's fury has become seismic. She has literally gone underground, raging again, VIA LIVE SATELLITE, as Mount St. Helens. The woman seated next to me asks if I am feeling all right. I nod, just as I had when watching Hurricane Jeanne. "That's my mother." I smiled, pointing to the volcano on CNN. I mentioned her sudden death. I explained that she had been a hurricane, but now, "She's spewing ash because she's very angry and not ready to go."

"The woman did not think I was crazy," I told Brenda. "Then this lovely woman said something so simple and beautiful."

Hot fat tears started rolling down my cheeks.

Mike leaned over and put his hand on my shoulder.

Samantha came over, put her arms around me, then silently returned to her chair.

Jim smiled very sweetly and said, "I want to know what the lady on the plane said and I promise not to hug you."

"The woman turned out to be a Baha'i," I said. "Rather than dismiss me as crazy, her eyes filled with tears and this tiny flash flood made me feel less alone. Complete strangers often help me through the most difficult moments in my life. She made me feel connected to a larger empathy. 'Sometimes life's a wick that burns slowly,' the woman said, 'but sometimes the wind can blow the candle out suddenly.'"

"That's beautiful," Ann said softly.

Pat buried her face in her hands and bowed her head.

"A sudden, unexpected, and tragic loss is different from a loss you can prepare for." Brenda said.

"I had a bit of both," Jim said softly. "I took care of Stew for five years, then found him hanging from a beam in our living room."

"ALS was torture," Pat whispered. "Sorry, Jim and Brenda, I don't mean to interrupt."

"Brian died fast and far away," Samantha said. "I'm so grateful he wasn't alone."

"For those of you who don't know," Brenda said,

"Brian was a Navy Seal and we thank him for his service."

"I wish I could say my husband was honorable," Cheryl said. "I gave him my kidney." She hesitated, then closed her eyes. "After he died, I found out he'd been cheating on me for 40 years." She opened her eyes and added, "I want my fucking kidney back."

I went from sobbing to chewing on my cheek lining to keep from laughing. This was ladylike Cheryl's first and splendidly honest revelation. Then I did this weird pivot and found myself saying with Brenda-like Zen, "It's complicated when you find out posthumously that your spouse was a liar, a cheat, pathological, or left you in a mountain of debt."

"Juliette is not here to mourn her husband," Pat said, with Brenda listening protectively, "because Nick deliberately blew up their home, killing himself and their new puppy. So the kindest thing I can say is that I am certain he had a first-class ticket to hell. We all mourn the loss of their innocent puppy."

"Why would anybody do that!?" Macy of Hugh Michael fame asked.

"We're getting a bit far afield," Brenda said.

"With all due respect, Macy," Jim added, "the 'why?' question is still the first, the last, and the constant question I get about Stew's suicide, and it still upsets me because it's the wrong question."

"What's the *right* question?" Samantha asked. She really wanted to know.

"There's no question other than, 'How can I help?'" Brenda suggested, "or 'What can we do to prevent this epidemic of depression and suicide?'"

"I agree," Pat said. "I've registered to march in this year's Out of the Darkness walk. I also want to clarify that Nick was not depressed. He was a calculating nut job."

I gave Pat the evil eye and stepped on her toe, which means *Shut up, I can do my own talking.*

Mike was fidgeting in his chair so badly it was tipping. He abandoned the folding chair and grabbed the only stationary chair in the room, but even the armchair could not contain him. "Jim's right. There is no 'why' and Brenda's right. It's the wrong question. What's more, I lied to all of you." He stood up, pacing. "My daughter's death has been so unbearable that I could not handle the additional stigma of *What kind of parent would allow hard drugs?* You get more sympathy if you say 'accidental overdose' than if you say 'heroin addict or meth addict,'" he said. "My beautiful, kind, brilliant daughter was a heroin addict."

He was heading out the door when Brenda stood up.

"Mike," she said firmly. "And this applies to all of you. I insist that you ignore whatever shame or expectations you and society hold. It's a matter of education, even in a bereavement group. I'm urging you to stay. You are safe here."

Mike came back and sat down and we let out a collective sigh of relief...until Ann almost triggered a bereavement group mutiny by saying, "Everything happens for a reason."

"For what reason, *exactly*, does everything happen?" Macy asked Ann.

"I know that Ann is trying to be helpful," I said. "I know that she is a kind person who has suffered one

of the worst losses possible, but honestly, when my mother was sick, I could not tolerate hearing *Everything happens for a reason* in the detached, breezy manner my supermarket checker says *Have a nice day*.
"

"It's a matter of faith," Ann said.

"I'm a woman of faith," Cheryl said. Her hands were clasped, revealing an impeccable manicure. "But I can't find any good *reason* for any of our losses."

"I don't share Ann's faith in some divine reason," Mike said. "But I think she's very lucky to have it."

Before my mother died, people made other pat statements like "This is an impossible situation." (As if I didn't know). They would ask what they could do. Some would define, very specifically, what they could or could not do. If they could not help, they'd suggest, "Can't you hire someone to sleep in the hospital with her?" Many said they were "not good at caregiving." Others simply showed up and did what was obviously needed. My aunt prevented my father from setting fire to the house (he always forgot to turn off the tea kettle). Another domestic hero flipped the oxygen back on when my father would routinely turn it off, insisting he did not need it.

The "Everything happens for a reason" crowd sucked up a lot of phone time, always when I was too exhausted to either receive or formulate words. What I needed were bodies on site. My mother knew this. She had barely survived a major operation, yet her first words coming out of anesthesia had been, "Who's at home with your father?" After my mother's death, the "Everything happens for a reason" people were mercifully silent. I take that to mean that either their world-view was working for them, or it was not.

"I've had a crisis of faith ever since Brian died in Iraq," Samantha confessed.

"Your faith is being tested," Ann said.

"*The Celestine Prophesy* was a bestseller that popular-ized 'Everything Happens for a Reason,'" Macy said. "It continues to be checked out of our library regularly."

Brenda nodded. "Thank you, Macy. There's no doubt the book helps a lot of people."

Jim brought up another issue that rankled many of us, namely, the false intimacy of end-of-life profession-als. "What kind of casket *would Stew prefer?*" Jim said, imitating the smarmy funeral home director.

"What color casket would *Mom* like?" I added.

"At the graveyard," Pat said, "they asked me 'Does Jordan prefer the sun or the shade?'"

Mike guffawed, then apologized to Pat, though all of us had either smacked our hands over our mouths to cover a smile or smother a giggle.

"How did you reply?" Ann asked Pat.

I held my breath, certain Pat would say, "Jordan's dead; he doesn't give a shit."

"I told him to ask Jordan," Pat said.

I burst out laughing. Even Brenda smiled.

Mike said, "Our church organist asked if my daughter would prefer a traditional hymn or a Negro spiritual."

We looked up.

"So I asked if he knew any Amy Winehouse or Janis Joplin and that's what he played!"

"A man I had never met appeared from behind the

lilies at Bob's funeral," Cheryl said quietly, then raised her voice with indignation. "He handed me his card and said, 'Call me. I'm an attorney specializing in medical malpractice.'"

Everyone in the group had his or her version of End of Life Professionals. Samantha offered the only positive experience. A military escort had accompanied her husband's flag-draped coffin from Dover Air Force Base and sat with her in a quiet place while she opened the pouch containing Brian's personal effects—a watch, his dog tags, and a medallion of St. Christopher.

Pat covered her face with her hands again and lowered her head.

Brenda asked if she was all right.

"I thought I was," Pat said. "I came to Oregon to help Juliette find a place to grieve, but I find myself missing my husband. He was such a good man and a good husband. And I'm worried about saying that, now that I've violated Juliette's privacy by telling you what a scumbag her husband was and now that we all know Cheryl would kill her husband all over again to get her kidney back."

Cheryl laughed aloud. She was always so reserved, contained, and perfectly groomed that it moved us to see her jump up and throw her arms around Pat, mildly displacing what seemed to be her blonde wig. "You're all helping me so much."

My father was the wick that burned (very) slowly. I waited my entire life for the dreaded call. He battled lung cancer for 40 years, somehow outliving his surgeon and burying his wife. Mom barely outlived her own mother, who died two months before her. Her mother had lived to 101. By our calculation, Mom had thirty more years. She would enjoy good health in the company of her daughter and grandchildren. In this genetically incontestable scenario, my father would have gone first. No longer would she sit by him, as he slept, untangling 50 feet of oxygen tubing and securing the plastic prong that sometimes slipped out of his nose. No longer would she have to sleep with her clothes on in the event of a call to 911.

The only blessing is that they were gone before Nick blew up our house. That surely would have killed them.

Part 2 - June

Father

Collector of Moments

8

LOVE LETTERS

The good news is that in Lake Oswego nobody gives you the finger, even after you cause a three-car pileup. When waiting to make a left turn, few people honk you into oncoming traffic.

You don't get the misplaced rage.

The bad news is that I'm bored. There's no Edge here. Only Laid Back. Militantly Laid Back. Pat, Bill, and I tried to make a list in defense of Edge, but it was a very mixed bag. Some ties. Some clear victories for Laid Back.

Edge RSVPs. Laid Back doesn't even show up.

Edge returns phone calls. Laid Back does not.

Edge chops down trees to receive badly needed light. Laid Back makes it a criminal offense.

Edge keeps psychiatrists in business. Laid Back
does not.

Edge has restaurants with New-York-Minute service.
Laid Back reassures customers that baby lettuce did not
suffer when it met its forager.

Edge produces better hair stylists and colorists. Laid
Back grows out gray.

Edge is competitive. Laid Back is laid back.

Edge gets you fired. Laid Back gets you fired (*tie score*).

Edge causes war. Laid Back does not.

Edge causes multiple car collision pileups. Laid Back
does not.

Edge produces white-collar criminals who live in
luxury homes. Laid Back produces sociopaths who live
in cabins.

Edge produces art. Laid Back produces crafts.

Edge wears stilettos. Laid Back wears Birkenstocks
with socks.

Edge is arrogant and compiles lists like this. Laid Back
is too relaxed and enjoying life to bother.

The only thing Laid Backs are not laid back about is

assisted suicide. They changed its name to Death with Dignity.

One more. Edge creates jobs. Laid Back does not.

I applied for a second job at Lewis and Clark in the law school library to supplement our income. In addition to my Masters in Education, I developed a working knowledge of legal research during my divorce. Not half as much as Carol Vesuvius Schell, but enough to be an assistant librarian. Pat is especially hopeful because Lewis and Clark has distinguished itself in the field of Animal Law. While on sabbatical in my house (Mother's Day + 18), she's used the library to research her third act and narrowed her search down to The Animal Legal Defense Fund and the National Disaster Animal Response Team.

Lucas is pulling weeds and mowing the lawn as a thank you for practicing baseball with Joey. By doing so, he knows I will no longer apply the weed killer, Round-Up.

Bill, meanwhile, plays baseball with the kids and Pat cheer-plays alongside them. Joey has made virtually no progress at either catching or throwing the ball.

I am watching them through the window, sorting through the belongings I shipped to Oregon. Every incision I make with the retractable box cutter tortures me with the content it reveals. Pat tells me that some people can't take it. They hire companies to do it for them. I wonder how this works. Do hired hands come in with pair after pair of dispassionate eyes and system-atically pack, load up, and dispense of memories? Anything of value, of course, can be sold. Memories have no market value, which is precisely why the professionals can be efficient with letters and photographs that leave me paralyzed with grief.

Lucas pivots the mower in front of the window. He doesn't strike me as the sort of man who stops a lawn-mower to comfort a woman. I wonder if Bill is differ-ent. I feel alone, yet somehow comforted by the melancholy that suffuses Orhan Pamuk's book, which reminds me that I have yet to thank Macy for lending it to me. According to Pamuk, the melancholy of Istanbul is *huzun*, a Turkish word whose Arabic origins combine a feeling of deep spiritual loss and anguish with a hopeful way of looking at life. Right now, Pamuk helps me understand that people are feeling the *saudade* of Lisbon, the *tristeza* of Burgos, the *mufa* of Buenos Aires, the *mestizia* of Turin, the *Traurigkeit* of Vienna, and the *glumness* of Glasgow.

I don't want to bother Pat with all this because, honestly, I don't want Bill to participate. I only want to be with people who knew and loved my parents.

My father labeled all our photographs so carefully. Manila dividers in index card files. Canada, 1957; World's Fair, 1964; The West, 1979; Europe 1988. The slides rest in aluminum boxes, fresh as on the day they came back from Kodak. Our trip to Yosemite is still in the carousel. In the desk he built to house the slides and photographs, he'd stacked reel after reel of 8 mm film, followed by reel upon reel of Super 8 film. Inside another cabinet, beige and brown projectors stood ready to play the movies. He kept all our projectors and, when the technology changed, he used a VHS recorder to edit in-house transfers of film to tape. By the time CDs and DVDs emerged, my father's memory loss was too great to make sense of what, under normal circumstances, would have been a routine challenge.

What will I do with this time capsule of audio-visual equipment?

What will I do with all their things?

If I don't do anything, their lives won't stick.

Do my parents stick in anyone else's heart as much as mine? They outlived many of their friends, so I have no way of knowing. For those who remain, I have no way of reaching them. This saddens me. Their friends would care. They would want to know.

I am heartsick to the point of wondering why anyone takes pictures. What's the point? Who will collect them? My mother spent most of her adult life keeping perfect files for my report cards, my test scores, my certificate of baptism, and my college diploma. It's all here. The letters from summer camp. My parents' letters to each other. Pictures of them in Paris. My beautiful mother is smiling next to a gargoyle on Notre Dame. My father is a lieutenant stationed in Germany. My father hopping a freight train to escape the summer heat in New York City.

I never read my parents' letters out of respect, so it feels sinful to keep them.

All that time my mother spent finishing her work at

home, sorting, copying, filing, when I was so lonely for her company.

I am still lonely for her company.

Which is another reason I don't want to do this. I want to be with my children. And Lucas needs me to make a decision about moss. He thinks he is making me happy by talking about herbicides. He has offered to take me to Mexico. He thinks I need a change of air. I tell him that I am *not* wallowing in grief; I am sad. On days like today, sadness is a fume which follows me everywhere.

Grace appears in the doorframe, her pink sweatpants covered in grass stains. She drops her hot-pink mitt and sits down next to me. "Who's that handsome man?" She points to the picture of my father on the freight train. "He has my eyes," she says.

Should I throw the files away?

Would my mother shred them?

Should I make a bonfire and burn everything?

My mother might not want a bonfire. She favored burial. They insisted on being buried together, but my father was *cremated*—a verb so revoltingly palatable it makes my stomach turn.

I take a break to get the mail. I can smell our freshly cut grass and hear Sam laughing as Bill pitches and Pat repeatedly fails to hit the ball.

Lily's mother retrieves her mail from our bank of communal mailboxes.

"Thank you for being a second family to Jackie," she says.

"We love Jackie," I said. "Thanks for signing for all my deliveries last week."

Lily's mother, Mrs. Jenny Anderson, is trying to be nice, but in my mind she is still the mother of a midget white supremacist.

"Are you okay?" she asks.

"No, actually," I said, pulling one utility bill and a stack of coupons from the mailbox. "I'm going through my parents' belongings. That's what's in the boxes you signed for."

"I'm sorry," she said, patting my shoulder. "It's rough. My husband went through it. You'll be fine."

I'm not fine.

It occurs to me that millions of people go through the day *not* thinking how I think, *not* feeling how I feel. And I envy them. Because they have lost people they love, and *they are fine*. Imagine that.

Half an hour later, surrounded by box after box of concentrated misery, Bill walks in. The last person on earth I want to see. Looking him in the eye would be easy had I kept my fat mouth shut at the Los Angeles Airport. Everything I say or feel towards Bill as Pat's boyfriend is mired and marred by awkwardness and humiliation. I have never had a romantic overlap with my best friend, nor do I intend to. I pride myself for *not* being the woman other women have to worry about. To be clear: Pat and I are not interested in the same men, nor have we ever slept with the same man. This is true of all of my girlfriends.

Bill sits down on the spot of carpet recently vacated by Gracie. I cannot figure out if he is radiating a great deal of Cooperstown heat or if I am. He is holding a book, which I assumed was about the latest technology in retinal scans. He pulled out the bookmark—a postcard of Pieter Brueghel's *Landscape with the Fall of Icarus*.

"My wife gave me this."

On the back, she had written W. H. Auden's poem. *About suffering they were never wrong, The Old Masters...*

"Your *wife*?"

"Yes."

"Um. Does Pat know about your wife?"

"Yes."

I had not read Auden's "Musée des Beaux Arts" since college. Since masterpieces are wasted on binge-drinking, drug-addled undergraduates, I gave it my full attention, despite my unrelenting curiosity regarding Bill's marital status.

In Breughel's Icarus, *for instance: how everything*
turns away
Quite leisurely from the disaster; the plowman may
Have heard the splash, the forsaken cry,
But for him it was not an important failure; the sun shone
As it had to on the white legs disappearing into the green
Water; and the expensive delicate ship that must have seen
Something amazing, a boy falling out of the sky,
had somewhere to get to and sailed calmly on.

"I thought you might want to see this," he said, handing me the postcard. "People were going on with their lives, uninterrupted by the boy's drowning." He pointed to the boy's skeleton-white legs disappearing into the green water. "Some of us would have changed course to rescue the child," he said. "I want you to know, Juliette, that you can count on me if you need anything."

"Thank you, Bill," I said quietly. "That's very kind of you." I handed him back the postcard. "Your wife has exquisite taste."

"Had," he said. He gently turned over the postcard to examine Brueghel's painting. "I'll let you get on with your task," he said. He pressed his strong, warm hand against mine and carefully tucked the postcard back inside his book.

Then he stood up and left.

That night I lay in bed remembering my father's garage. His workbench now silent and eerily neat; the saws, the mallets and I-Beam levels. As if standing guard, pliers, screwdrivers, and spring clamps hung from the pegboard. In the drawers, boxes were filled with nails and screws, a size for every task. Dozens of patch cords in Ziploc bags. Plugs and cables I did not understand. Issues of polarity, current, and compatibility. An entire army of tools awaited the return of its commander.

A palette rested on his easel, the oil paint dry. The final colors he would use: Cobalt Violet, Hooker's Green, Raw Umber, Cadmium Red and Burnt Sienna.

If I don't sift through our family's history, who will know the difference? Who will care? What should I save? What should I throw into a bag for Goodwill? Collectors always find their place in history. How else do Tupperware collections arrive at the Smithsonian?

Letter to the Afterlife

Dearest Father,
What do you want me to do with your love
letters? Out of respect for your privacy (and
Mom's), I have not read them, and I do not
intend to.

Sam and Grace's digital generation might not
have love letters as we know them; no handwriting on paper; no postcard to finger with love
and longing. A tear splotch on a love letter is a
memory, but a single teardrop on a laptop
keyboard can short the circuit and erase
everything.

They won't know what they're missing. Or will
the process of grieving be far less painful?

Love,
Juliette

9

SMALL PLEASURES

I got the job (Oh, Happy Day!) at Lewis and Clark (Oh, Happy Day!) When I can wash (When she can wash) my crushing debts away.

I start next Wednesday, after the bereavement group. Once a week, with the likelihood of additional hours. Wednesday is our school district's half day. Grace has soccer after school and Sam's got baseball practice. As if all this were not enough to make my heart explode, tomorrow is Poetry Day in my fourth-grade class.

I usually start with limericks or Robert Burns and have my students fill in the blanks:

O my Luve is like a (ADJECTIVE), red (NOUN)
That's newly sprung in (PROPER NOUN);
O my (NOUN) is like the (NOUN)
That's (ADVERB) played in tune.

Which invariably ends up something like this (from last year):

O my Luve is like a STINKY, red BUNNY
That's newly sprung in HALLOWEEN;
O my ZOMBIE is like the PORTAPOTTY
That's LOUDLY played in tune.

My fourth graders always lobby for penis and vagina as nouns, but teachers have to consider the parents.

As a parent, myself, I cannot wait to hear what Sam and Grace recite in class. Sam would rather play Barbies with his archenemy, Lily, than memorize a poem, but he's agreed to work with Bill to find one he likes. "It's a surprise," he insists. Grace is rehearsing with Pat, but I'm not allowed to hear her choice.

I knocked on Pat's door to remind her that we were running late for Ann's school fundraiser, which Pat committed us to attending. Bill offered to watch the kids.

"Do you have the address?" I asked Pat, pulling out of the driveway in my Ford Fiesta.

"23 Pinewood Road."

"That's not it."

"Says it right here."

I pulled over, a bit irritated that Pat wasn't taking full responsibility for an event she volunteered me to attend and grabbed the piece of paper she was holding. She had printed out the email, highlighted the address in neon yellow, and written the name of the "Small Pleasures" co-host.

"*FUCK!*"

"What?"

"That's Lucas's house."

"Oh, wow." A smile began curling at the edge of her mouth. She was already imagining the dramatic possibilities. "I had no idea."

"I don't want to go." I made a sharp U-turn.

"We *promised.*"

"YOU promised."

"The whole point of the bereavement group is that we're supposed to be supporting each other."

"This is extracurricular. Carol scares the shit out of me."

"It's helping Ann honor Jake!" Pat said. In response to my erratic driving, she lowered her voice. "By the way, how does that witch know Ann?"

"Her son must have gone to Palisades."

When Pat and I pulled up to Carol's house, Lucas was clearing sports gear out of their garage. Carol was waving her arms in protest.

"I didn't know you were coming." He brightened.

"Why is Carol flailing her arms?" I asked.

"She doesn't want her clients to see me move out," Lucas said. He appeared quite serious until he noticed that Pat and I were sporting matching chenille bathrobes.

"What are you wearing!?" He laughed. His eyes descended to the bosomy triangle framed by my robe's collar.

"It's a 'Small Pleasures' spa party fundraiser for Palisades," I said, pinching my collar shut.

"I didn't know your wife was the co-host," Pat sighed. "I'm in the doghouse."

"That makes two of us," he said. Then he rested his left hand on my arm. "Notice anything?"

"You took your ring off," Pat said. She does not miss a trick.

Lucas saw Carol greeting her first guests at the door. "Gotta go," he said.

"Where?" I asked.

"To my new apartment. I'm renting month to month. We'll see how it goes."

"Do Mia and Joey know?"

"Sort of."

"What does that mean?"

"We told them I needed a place in downtown Portland for work, but that nothing would change for them."

Carol was made up like a geisha. "All with SusieQ products!" she cried in a secretive whisper. I almost sang, *You great big beautiful doll.*

Fifteen mothers from Palisades Elementary School milled around the dining room table in bathrobes, choosing their color palette. The spa party fundraiser had morphed into a SusieQ Cosmetics sales convention. Carol announced that SusieQ is going head-to-head with Mary Kay in Portland.

Pat is thrilled. This evening is turning into the makeover she's always wanted me to have.

At eight o'clock in the evening, with nowhere to go afterwards, Pat and I found ourselves exfoliating, plumping our lips, choosing a scent (Happy) and picking out our color palette. Most of the mothers chose Jazz. It was the recommended palette for women with blonde hair and blue eyes. Carol made it simple. The only other color palettes were for a person with grey hair (Charm); for a brunette (Unique); or for a person of color (Exotic).

I chose Unique.

Pat picked Exotic.

"I'm not sure that's the appropriate choice for you," Carol said.

"Why not?" Pat asked.

"Because you are not a person of color."

"But I'm not a brunette. I'm an auburn."

"We don't have that kind of flexibility."

"Juliette's not a brunette and she picked Unique."

"That's different."

"Why?"

"Because we don't have any more Jazz palettes left."

"Correct. And you have plenty of Exotic left because there's not a single person of color in Lake Oswego."

"Are you trying to get Juliette in trouble for picking Unique?"

"No. I know for a fact that Juliette is unique because she is my best friend. And I'm not in trouble," Pat smiled. "I'm simply Exotic."

"Fine," Carol said, with a winning smile, because *who wants to lose a customer?!* "But you are not correct when you say that there is not a single person of color in Lake Oswego. Lucas and I adopted a brown one and Juliette has two of them."

I looked up from the Exotic palette to see Carol

wink at me by way of endearing herself as a professional now, rather than, say, an ignorant leather-faced
treadmill assassin. She looked tired and for a moment I
felt sorry for her, knowing what lay ahead for her and
the children. But when she said, "I'm okay with your
interest in Exotic because, let's face it, our kids are
awfully tan!"

"My kids are mixed," I said firmly, putting a stop to
her chummy twinning. "They are German-Indian-
Franco-Irish Americans and your daughter, Mia, is
from Guatemala."

Macy arrived late in full Goth armor. Carol, who
had never met Macy and who knew even less about her
loss than our bereavement group, appeared relieved to
see someone who looked genuinely different. She
seized the opportunity to demonstrate her product's
flexibility.

"Macy is borderline Exotic," Carol announced,
cheerfully.

"What does that make Ginny?" Pat had just received
a delightfully easy Korean barbecue recipe from her.

"Ginny is Asian. She isn't white and she isn't brown."
She smiled at Ginny. "As I said, we don't have that much
flexibility."

"Thank God she didn't say Ginny was yellow," Macy
whispered to Ann, who snorted in amusement and
thanked her for coming.

Carol is not alone in her racial profiling. In our
neighborhood, people don't always distinguish between
countries of origin. Hence, you're either brown or
white. Melting pot be damned: If you live in any suburb
in America that has spawned generation after genera-

tion of its own, you can be from Sicily, Syria, Sri Lanka, Israel, India, Turkey, Peru, Mexico and, bingo, you're a "brown one."

Things only got worse.

Ginny noticed that Macy was Modified. The makeup artist complimented Macy on her tattoo: "What a lovely gargoyle." Macy thanked her, saying she was lucky to live in a fairly liberal area, where library patrons are not offended by her tattoos, if they could even see them. "In more conservative towns, librarians have to conceal their modifications involving tongues, nipples, or genital piercings."

"That's disgusting," Ginny said.

"You'd be amazed how good it feels," Ann said.

Many of the mothers were riveted. They formed a fluffy-robe perimeter around Macy and Ann—all beautiful, all perfectly made-up, all refilling their wine glasses for the second or third time, all expecting to hear tale after tale of sexual depravity, debauchery, and pleasure.

Carol, who had not drunk a single drop of alcohol, favoring instead her prescription medication, looked horrified.

Ann admitted that, in addition to the genital piercing, she had once had a 10-gauge barbell on her tongue and a 14-gauge captive bead in her nipple.

"Stop!" Carol said. Her saleswoman smile collapsed.

Standing at five foot ten and weighing at least 225 pounds, Ann is a big girl. I did not want to think about any part of her anatomy. If this fundraiser goes to hell because of Ann's revelations, we'll chalk it up to Everything Happens for a Reason.

"My husband misses the barbell, but he insisted I remove it for Jake's private school interview." Ann wiped away a tear, smearing the corner of her Unique eye. "I refused, so that's how Jake ended up at Palisades, which turned out to be a perfect fit. I'm so grateful to the school. That's why I'm here."

When Ann poured herself a third glass of wine, Carol locked the wine credenza. As if on cue, the makeover specialist who had complimented Macy on her gargoyle rushed over to correct Ann's sad, raccoon smear and introduced the more polite subject of her child's various diagnoses. She commiserated with a Jazz Palate mom about her son's Attention Deficit Hyperactivity Disorder (ADHD). She said that her son had similar issues, along with a sensory disorder. He can only wear nylon sports clothes, and briefs are out of the question. On and on she went about dozens of tests performed, the results, and the nights she stayed up worrying.

Jazz's son very clearly has ADHD. He not only has the attention problems; he also has impulse control problems. I know the teacher who asked Jazz's son why he was making animal sounds in class. He said, "I don't know." My colleague asked him if he made them at home. He said, "No." She asked him to stop. He said, "I can't."

The makeover specialist finished Ann's eye makeup, gave her a hug, then pulled a product out of her bag, perky as the twins in the old Doublemint Gum ads, and said, "This solved everything."

"What is it?" Jazz asked. Another fluffy-robe caucus

convened, this time for the mothers of children with ADHD.

"A SusieQ topical cream with active herbs," she whispered. "It dramatically reduced my son's symptoms." The makeover specialist sounded unnaturally composed and pious, like a cult member. Jazz was not convinced that any balm or aroma therapeutic compound could calm that fabulous circus in her son's brain or those impulses that fly off, with no surge protection whatsoever.

"It retails for $19.99."

The makeover specialist pulled a few tubes out of her bag and waved them at Jazz, with the same bleached smile as her SusieQ leader, Carol.

In the presence of so many SusieQ disciples, Jazz confided to Pat that she could never use the word medication; nor could she speak candidly about her son's condition, especially since he was responding well to low doses of Ritalin. But under what felt like enormous pressure to conform to a group of underemployed mothers hustling their own products, Jazz bought two 4-ounce tubes of the putatively miraculous aroma therapeutic homeopathic cream, *Serenity*.

Carol was so moved by the response to her new line of medical creams that she pulled a new product out of her bag. It was a nutritional gluten-free protein drink that was still in trial. "Joey has Asperger's," she said. "We've already noticed an improvement."

I am certain that Lucas would not agree.

A smaller makeover caucus convened, made up of mothers whose children had Asperger's or High-Functioning Autism.

That evening, Carol increased her net worth by ten thousand dollars, 75 percent of which she generously donated to Palisades Elementary.

Pat, Macy, and I stayed late to help Ann clean up. Carol spent most of her time in the bathroom. Lucas was still outside, loading ski equipment and his mountain bike into an SUV. His move coincided with Carol's request for more room in the garage for her SusieQ product lines. In addition to the new Asperger's drink, Carol was developing a series of calming teas for both Prader-Willi Syndrome and various Obsessive-Compulsive Disorders.

Upstairs in the den, Joey and his sister were watching *The Alfred Hitchcock Hour*, which Carol ordered from the library. I walked in on the episode where the father tries to murder the mother. I grabbed the remote and turned off the television.

"Mom told us to watch this!" Mia said.

"Even if he kills her, they use ketchup for blood in black-and-white films," Joey said.

"I'll tell your mother I switched it." I scanned their *Veggie Tales* collection and saw *Get Smart*. "Joey, are you a *Get Smart* kind of kid?"

"Yes."

"I like Agent 99," Mia smiled. "I want to be like her. Max is stupid."

"*Get Smart* it is!"

When Pat and and I took out the trash, we saw a woman walking her Shih Tzu. The Shih Tzu's severe underbite did not deter it from barking at a skunk, who favored us by holding back his arsenal, given the suffo-cating blanket of air already present from his natural musk. Bad haircut, chunky body, sensible shoes, the woman carried a transistor radio whose scratchy blare dulled her battery of percussive farts.

"If I end up like her, put a gun to my head," I said.

"Me first," Pat said.

Lucas was inside, saying goodnight to the children. Joey complained that he had a "skunk headache." He claimed it hurt "like an ice-cream headache."

Lucas kissed Mia and Joey goodnight. "Go to bed," he said.

They lobbied for one more episode of *Get Smart.*

"No deal," Lucas said. "Where's your mother?"

"She's in the bathroom puking," Mia said.

"Must have been the canapés," Pat said, as we entered the den.

"What are canapés?" Joey asked.

Lucas looked towards Pat and me, pleading for a definition.

"Canapés are finger-sized appetizers," Pat said.

"I'll go check on her," he said. When he gave Mia and Joey especially long hugs, my heart was breaking for everyone involved.

Letter to the Afterlife

Chere Grandmere,

I went to a party with Pat, which required me to wear makeup and I started thinking about your hair salon in Paris. All those women you made beautiful during the War. They told you their stories; still, they kept secrets. One turned out to be a collaborator. All that time you spent on Madame Pruneau's hair. How could you have known that, after the Liberation of Paris, they would make an example of her by shaving her head?

I wish you could make an example of Carol, the mother who hosted tonight's fundraiser. She referred to Mia, the little girl she adopted from Guatemala, as a "brown one," along with your two "brown" great grandchildren.

I still have your clippers.

Bisous,
Juliette

Letter to the Afterlife

Dears Mom and Dad,

You continue to make things hard for me because you had a very good marriage.

Down here, I see the following types of marriages:

Miserable Sexless Marriages
Happy Sexless Marriages
Happy Open Marriages

Miserable Open Marriages
Happy Childless Marriages
Miserable Childless Marriages

(and this is somewhat related to...)

Wonderful mothers who are terrible wives
Horrible mothers who are wonderful wives
Wonderful fathers who are terrible husbands
Terrible fathers who are wonderful husbands

You both fall into a rare, dual category: loving spouses and wonderful parents.

I've had an impossibly good example.

Love,
Juliette

10

TEACH YOUR CHILDREN WELL

Taupe metal folding chairs all lined up along the wall of Sam's fourth-grade class. Pat, Bill, and I, along with Grandpa Chola and Grandma Kristina are sitting in the front row waiting for him to recite his poem. His grandparents have flown in from California to celebrate his 10th birthday. Sam's wearing a red flannel shirt and khaki pants. When he points to a picture of the universe projected on the class whiteboard, he looks professorial.

"The Hubble took this picture from space," Sam says. "I turned the official statement from NASA into a poem."

Most of the elements
in the human body
were created
in the inferno
of a burning star

"Oh, my!" Pat exclaimed. "That's gorgeous."

Grandma and Grandpa beamed with pride.

Bill started the clapping, which was robust.

I joined in, as did the other parents and students. Joey raised his hand and their teacher, Miss Bundy, called on him.

"That was really good, Sam."

"Thanks, Joey."

Miss Bundy smiled. "What a perfect 'found poem,' Sam!"

I turned to Bill and tried not to gaze at him adoringly. "Thank you," I said, "Brilliant."

He briefly clasped my hand. "It was Sam's idea," he said.

I could see Lucas scorching Bill's hand with his eyes. I turned to Pat, worried that she would think something untoward of all this pattycake, but my heart melted when I saw her mouthing the words *great job!* to Sam.

After Sam's poetic collaboration with NASA, I raced to Grace's class, with Sam, Pat, Bill, and her grandparents in tow. I was grateful not to be sitting alone, which is usually the case for a displaced single mother. Each child averages eight family members: two parents, two sets of grandparents, one aunt and uncle, and/or therapy dog. To compensate for my children's lack of representation, I often clap *way too loudly* according to Sam and Grace, which makes things even more painful and awkward for them and doubly-so for me, given that many family members know me as the fourth-grade teacher at Bellemont.

Once seated, Pat waved to Grace, who scanned her audience before reciting:

This Be the Verse
by Philip Larkin

They fuck you up, your mum and dad.
They may not mean to, but they do.
They fill you with the faults they had
And add some extra, just for you.

I turned to Pat, who was grinning at her protégé.

This is hardly the first time Pat's lessons have gone on behind my back or even under my nose. Last year my son was grappling with an eternal mystery for a young scientist. I'd been chatting with Pat online when he came in and asked if I'd deactivate parental controls to let him continue important research. When I said it was too late, he shot a question to Pat directly. "I understand the stuff about the sperm and the egg," he said, "but how does the sperm *get* to the egg?"

Instead of saying, "Ask your mother," and before I could say, "That's a very good question," Pat told him she'd overnight a book that would answer all his questions. The following evening Grace raced downstairs, marched up to me, short of breath and face flushed. "Sam is reading a disgusting book with pictures of a penis stuck in a vagina." *Where Kids Come From* lay on his floor, open to the chapter, "The Incredible Swimming Sperm." The images were indisputably fallopian with a line drawing of a couple in the missionary position.

One of Grace's classmates muffled a nervous laugh, but the rest were shocked, including her third-grade teacher, Mrs. Mosen, and *especially* Grandma and Grandpa.

> But they were fucked up in their turn
> By fools in old-style hats and coats,
> Who half the time were soppy-stern
> And half at one another's throats.

By now, parental hands were thrashing the air as wildly as a feeding frenzy off Cannon Beach. Mrs. Mosen tried to calm the sea of opposition by lifting her right hand like a Pope about to speak. Lily's mother, Mrs. Jenny Anderson, stormed out.

"Grace, honey." Mrs. Mosen tried interrupting her, to no avail.

Pat had rehearsed my little girl so well that Grace was determined to finish with a flourish.

> Man hands on misery to man.
> It deepens like a coastal shelf.
> Get out as early as you can,
> *And don't have any kids yourself.*

Pat, Bill, and I were the only ones clapping until Sam gave Grace a standing ovation, which prompted Grandpa and Grandma to clap dutifully along with the rest of the audience, relieved the ordeal was over. Behind us, Lily mystified us by giving Grace a double thumbs up. Next to Mrs. Mosen, another pair of small hands started clapping. It was Mia, to Carol's pale-faced horror. Her distress was compounded when Joey's Aspergian rigidity shattered wide-open with a joyous display of unbridled laughter, which proved contagious. The entire third-grade class convulsed with laughter.

Despite Mrs. Mosen's increasingly desperate attempt at order, things only quieted down when Lily's mother, Mrs. Jenny Anderson, arrived with Mr. Barrow, the school principal. "The inmates are running the institution," he said to Mrs. Mosen, who had one year left before retirement. Because Mr. Barrow had recently been our principal at Bellemont, he recognized Grace as my daughter. Though twice interrupted by sputtering bursts of residual giggles, he finally was able to ask Grace why she chose "This Be the Verse."

Grace threw me an anxious look.

"Nice work, Pat," I said in a clenched whisper.

It wasn't entirely Pat's fault. Two months ago, on the way to soccer practice, Grace said, "I know a lot more than you think."

"I'm sure you do," I replied in the *listen don't react* voice modern parenting recommends.

"I know what a condom is!"

I was relieved we could check that item off the sex-ed list until Grace added, "It's a glove you put on your penis."

Why anyone would want to put a glove on his or her

penis was beyond me and it should have begged follow-up questions on Grace's part.

"What's your source?" I asked. When researching a topic on the Internet, I would teach my students about primary sources, but I cannot control the disinformation shared between children, distorted by a giant game of telephone, and broadcast to every small human in the elementary school.

"One of my friend's moms," Grace said, rightly protecting her source. "I also know what a tampon is."

"What's a tampon?"

"Don't *you* know!?"

"Yes, I do."

As if confiding something between us girls, she said, "It's a cigar-shaped Band-Aid that you stick up your vagina."

I must have look startled. Grace upped the ante.

"And *that's* how you lose your virginity."

"My mother's best friend read me the work of some English poets," Grace told Mr. Barrow. "This was my favorite."

"Why?"

"Because it's short, funny, and honest."

"Well, Grace," Mr. Barrow said, scanning the room, with his eyes landing on Mrs. Jenny Anderson. "I'm sure everybody here today will never forget the power of poetry and Philip Larkin," he said brightly.

Grandma Kristina astounded us with beautiful ringing laughter, as if circles of air and light were escaping from dark caves inside her.

"Not to say fuck," Grandpa Chola said softly, but he still gave Grace a hug.

Vesuvius came over, about to pop her cap, but Lucas, Joey, and Mia were so happy I tried to defuse Carol by placing an order for the new gluten-free protein drink she'd claimed worked wonders for Joey.

Even Mrs. Anderson, who saw Lily (now officially a *former* white supremacist) happy among her peers, came over and relented. "Unusual choice," she said to Grace, "but I do admire your courage."

Grace thanked her and I felt an instant rush of neighborly forgiveness.

That night, the sun melted like an orange marshmallow on the mountain behind our house. I had blinked so many times that when I closed my eyes, I saw dozens of polka dots on the cosmos of my palpebral screen.

For the first time since I can remember, I felt peaceful and content.

11

YURT A TROIS

For Sam's birthday, we promised to take him camping on Oregon's southern shore. We will be staying in a yurt, which is like Motel 6 without the TV.

Pat, Bill, Lucas, the kids, and I are lugging the camping gear from the parking lot on Highway 101 when I ask Bill point blank, "Are you sure you booked the yurts?"

"Yes, but I have to buy the Park Pass. I was going to ask you about that."

"I've got mine," Lucas offered.

Joey was so excited we could hear him singing, "Hi-Diddle-Dee- Dee–a camper's life for me!"

Sam could not stop interrupting and asking Bill questions about his work.

"What's your clearance?"

"Top Secret," Bill winked.

"Awesome," Sam said. "I just bought a spy set with my allowance."

"Do you play poker?" Sam asked.

"I'm from Texas," he said. "What do you think?"

"Seriously awesome," Sam nodded to himself. "This is going to be a great trip."

Sing Around the Campfire! Pat, Grace and Mia sang, *Join the Campfire Girls!*

"Despite her vocal prowess, Pat does not camp," I said. "Tell Bill the truth, Pat."

Two days earlier, Bill had showed Pat a picture of a yurt, which made her reconsider her promise to go camping. To allay her concerns, I took Pat, the kids, and their grandparents to OMSI, the Oregon Museum of Science and Industry, where they had devoted an entire room to the history of the yurts, known as *gers* to the Mongolians. Pat ducked in (the walls are five and a half feet tall) and, once inside, I heard her ask the other museum goers, "Where's the en suite?" By the time she emerged from the yurt, her cell phone was poised to make a reservation at the only four-star resort in Cannon Beach, the town closest to the campsite. "I prefer to stay somewhere with a key."

"That's where you come in, Juliette," Bill said. "I want you to show Pat the ropes."

"Juliette *does* have a point, Bill," Pat admitted. "I'm not much of a camper."

"See, now *that's* the kind of negative attitude that Lucas is talking about." Bill reached back to high-five Lucas.

At South Beach, we had finally ignited the barbecue when the fire department arrived, citing a new regulation deeming fire pits and barbecues a fire hazard.

"You might want to put up a sign," Bill said.

"They go up tomorrow," the firefighter said.

Pat complained about the campsite being too near the highway. "Truck traffic is not what I had in mind for ambient music."

Once again, we packed up our stoves, food, dishes, utensils, sleeping bags, and headed for Beverly Beach, where two yurt reservations opened up when the campers were a no-show. We enrolled Sam, Joey, Grace, and Mia in the Junior Ranger Program, which according to the brochure, will give them a sense of authority over their terrain and make them easier to parent.

For the rest of the day, we stared in wonder at the hundreds of seals, barking and wet, that lay varnished against the rocks in the late afternoon sun. When the sun finally set, Joey insisted that what we were seeing was not happening.

"Give it a rest, Joey," Lucas said.

"What does he mean?" Pat asked.

"Technically, the sun set five minutes ago, so what you're seeing is a sunset that already happened," Joey answered.

"You're so smart, Joey!" Pat said.

"He's so annoying," Grace said.

Lucas put his arm around his son and whispered, "Sometimes you've just got to watch it, enjoy it, and let others enjoy it, buddy."

After dinner, we roasted marshmallows and made s'mores. Sam was in his element, challenging Joey to duels with sticks picked clean of marshmallows.

When night fell, I gave the futons to the kids. Lucas and I took the bunk beds. I begged Pat and Bill not to put me in the same yurt as Lucas. Bill agreed to share the yurt with Lucas and the boys, but Pat said I was crazy.

"You've got to get on with your life," she said when the kids were out of earshot. "This is completely innocent and appropriate."

"I agree with Juliette," Bill said.

"Why?" Pat asked, "Don't you want to yurt with me?"

"It's awkward," I said.

"How does Lucas feel about it?" Pat asked.

"He's fine with it and we have an agreement."

"What kind of agreement?"

"The kids come first."

"How do the kids feel about it?" Pat asked.

"Thrilled."

"Case closed," Pat said.

That night, Joey complained about the crease in the futon, where it had been folded and unfolded too many times by too many campers. Lucas offered to have us take the futon, which was insanely forward on his part. I was wondering what had come over him when I heard murmurs of lovemaking from the neighboring yurt.

"What's that noise?" Mia asked.

"We're in the wild," I said. "Go to bed, honey."

"I can't. The animals make too much noise."

"I can't sleep either," Grace said.

"Well, get to bed now, because the animals wake up early and start all over again."

Lucas stifled a laugh.

The lovemaking from the neighboring yurt was getting more expressive. We could hear a woman moaning. Lucas suppressed another laugh-burst. "Is that Pat!?"

"Shut up," I whispered.

"Dad? Did Grace's mommy just tell you to shut up?"

"Yes, Mia. And I'll have to take her outside for a time out."

"I hear human animals," Joey said. "Are they having sex?"

Sam and Grace started to giggle.

"Go to bed," Lucas said in a voice devoid of authority.

Mia started drifting off to sleep, but Sam, Grace, and Joey giggled even more as the lovemaking reached a climax.

Lucas was unnerved in a manner I had never seen. When the kids finally fell asleep, he leaned over the bunk to see if I was awake, then he climbed down and pulled my hand.

"What are you doing?"

"Time for your Time Out."

I cupped my hand to whisper in his ear, but hit his mouth by mistake. Faster than a catfish catching live bait, he snatched a kiss. "Are you crazy? We can't leave the kids!"

"Yes, we can," he reassured me, grabbing a blanket off his bunk. "We'll be right behind our yurt."

The night air hung heavy with the moist incense of salt, moss, and loam. Even the moon looked sodden, casting a diffuse light, filtered by infinitesimal beads of water.

Lucas put his arm around my shoulder, then slipped it down to my waist, guiding me to the back of the yurt, where he stopped to tip my face towards his and met my eyes.

"It wasn't Pat," I said, confident that I'd detected nothing but tension between Pat and Bill and certain that my sexdar was perfectly calibrated.

"What?"

"Pat was not making those noises."

"Who cares?" He tipped my lips towards his and kissed me in that lingering way which leads to all things possible, impossible, and unstoppable.

"You are in violation of our Jamba Juice Agreement," I said, far less convincingly than I intended to.

"Objection," he whispered, laughing softly. "We're doing stuff with the kids and honoring Sam's birthday."

He caressed me in ways I did not think him capable. Lucas cradled my head and lay me on the blanket. His fingers pressed and somehow released every item I had just purchased in REI's blow-out sale. In this sheltered area, between the remains of an abandoned campfire, behind a bank of rosehip bushes, Lucas explored me so silently with a hunger so ravenously unlike him, that I was slow to hear what was, by then, the unmistakable sound of Pat and Bill's voices, far less playful than usual.

"You can't even smoke in this fucking park."

"*That's* Pat," I said.

When he chuckled, I shushed him.

I was feeling any snitty little nuisances dissolve into the purest pleasure by Lucas's touch. I had to believe that Lucas could hear Pat and Bill. If anything, their conversation seemed to goad him on, allowing him to express unprecedented levels of tenderness. Each time he heard Bill's voice, Lucas became more insistent in his desire to please. He was kissing me all over, very gently, but with increasing urgency and coaxing me in ways that made me—

"Come over here!" I heard Pat laugh.

"What is it?" Bill asked.

"Two teenagers fooling around where their parents cannot hear," Pat said. "Glad I don't have a daughter."

I felt Lucas's smile on my mouth, his silent performance geared to an invisibly present audience. "I want to make you—"

"Come over here!" Pat repeated.

They started arguing about accommodations. Pat was complaining about the bathrooms being too far. Something about the South Beach Hotel and Spa. Bill asked Pat to put out her cigarette.

Next came the rustling of leaves. I threw the blanket over my open buttons and zippers and any traces of skin. Lucas snatched a rusty frying pan from the ground to cover his nakedness. Pat was peering at us through the bushes, mouthing the word "SORRY!" when she saw me.

After Pat's hand released the rosehips, another hand parted the bush. By then, I had managed to conceal every inch of skin, but Bill stared at me with an intensity that penetrated the blanket. His eyes met mine. I turned away.

I do not owe Bill an explanation, certainly not *Mia and Lucas put me in a time out.*

"Juliette was right," Bill told Pat, as he stomped off. "You're not a camper."

Through the branches, I saw Pat thumbing a ride. A park ranger picked her up.

Bill entered the yurt and, with reality settling in, I noted the inequitable adult-child yurt ratio: Bill 1-0; Juliette/Lucas 2–4.

"Goddamn him," Lucas muttered, reaching for his clothes.

There was just enough light from the moon to catch a full glimpse of Lucas's naked body. I laughed quietly, resigned to the absurdity of the situation.

"What's so funny?" he snapped, balancing on one foot as he pulled his shorts on.

"Nothing," I said. "Beast that you are for dragging me out here, I was just admiring how well-equipped you are for mating in the wild."

We'd been so careful *not* to make noise that I froze at the sight of Mia, lying on her stomach, her little face propped between her fists.

"Did you get a time out?" she whispered in a voice hoarse with sleep.

"I sure did, Mia."

Satisfied that justice had been served, she rolled over and went back to sleep.

The next day, Bill made scrambled eggs for everyone, minus Pat.

I miss Pat. She would lighten the mood. That said, I'm angry she abandoned my boy on his birthday.

"You okay, Sam?" I asked. He looked a bit glum.

"Yeah. Where's Pat?"

"In a hotel. She's really not a camper."

"She promised me a kite," he said.

Lucas started singing *Kumbaya* in a voice so sleep deprived his baritone lowered to a bass. My mood had dropped an octave as well and my mind pursued a negative line of inquiry, wondering how Daddy Kumbaya could have married a woman who referred to sweet Mia as a "brown one." Though given the sudden deterioration of my marriage, I was in no position to judge.

Very few people in the throes of divorce (or even happily married) sing *Kumbaya*, which further made me worry that Lucas was out of touch. The ring was off, he had moved out, yet any good parent will do whatever he or she can do to rescue a marriage if there are children involved so, despite Lucas's loveless, sexless marriage, what if he cannot go through with a divorce? What if Carol's SusieQ Cosmetics (and her miracle cream empire) is a colossal failure and Lucas decides he'd rather deduct her Schedule C business losses from their joint tax returns than divorce her and maintain two households. The direction in which my tired, irritated mind was heading made me feel wobbly and unsafe.

Lucas eyed Bill, somewhat competitively, while flipping pancakes in a manner that defied the rules of simple aeronautics. He was making the children laugh, which made me smile until Grace eyed me accusingly.

"What's wrong?"

"Mia misses her mother."

Bill played Texas Hold 'em with Sam and Grace. He was unusually quiet.

To our horror, the Junior Ranger Program had been cancelled for the day, yet everyone was thrilled when it turned out to be a record day for collecting sand dollars.

Later that morning, Bill was nowhere to be found because he *can* check into hotels by himself, like Pat, or vanish, as he did, because he is not responsible for four children under the age of eleven.

At least Lucas gets *that*.

"Where's Bill?" the kids asked.

"He had to go back to work," Lucas said.

A shadow of discontent traveled over each face.

"Did he tell you that?" I wondered.

"He mentioned a security conference."

Grace pulled Lucas aside, after which he held Mia tenderly and looked over at me with a confused expression. I don't know what Grace is up to, but I am too busy re-configuring the rooming requirements of my guests. Grandma and Grandpa (Sam's Birthday + 2 days); Bill's stay (Memorial Day + 5 intermittent). I had just finished Pat (Mother's Day + 26 days and counting) when I heard her exuberant, throaty voice.

"Hello everybody!" Tall, lean, and majestic as the statue on the prow of a ship, her hair was flying and her huge smile indicated she'd had a glorious night's sleep. "What a *great* day for flying kites!"

"These are *so* cool!" Sam cried, as the kids ran over to inspect.

"I want the shark," Grace said.

"Birthday boy gets first pick," Pat said.

Sam chose the giant octopus, leaving the stingray for Joey, the box kite for Lucas and the diamonds for Mia, Pat, and me.

Grace got her shark.

BEREAVERS III

The Wednesday I was due to start work at Lewis and Clark, Macy almost got kicked out of our Bereavement Group, which I'd thought was impossible. She is upset. I am too.

Here's what happened: We went around the room, as we usually do.

Ann offered to start. She thanked those of us who had participated in the Palisades fundraiser and apologized for sharing too many kinky personal details that night. On her way to work the next day, she saw a teenage boy heading to the neighborhood skatepark, which reminded her of her son, Jake. "I lost it," she said. "I had to pull over."

"Would it help to change your route so you don't have to pass the skatepark?" Brenda asked.

"I tried," Ann said, "but something keeps pulling me back."

"I know what you mean," Mike said. "I'm beginning

to understand why people put up all those crosses by the side of the road."

"A shrine of sorts," Brenda suggested. "Does the skatepark serve as one for you?"

"Jake skated there all the time. It's the only ritual I have," Ann said. "I want to remember Jake every day because it would be worse to forget him."

"You will never forget him," Cheryl said.

"I would visit Brian's grave every day if I could," Samantha said.

"A sacred spot," Brenda said.

And this is what I like about the group. Nobody tells us to move on, to snap out of it, or tells us that it's only stress. When it was my turn, I told them that last year one of my work colleagues observed that I was losing weight.

"She asked me, 'Is it stress-related?'"

"I hate that word," Mike said.

"It's the medical buzzword of the 21st century," Jim said. He made us smile when he started mimicking an earnest health care provider. "Do you feel that being a gay male elevates your stress level?"

"What I'm experiencing has perfectly fine, old-fashioned words like sadness and sorrow," I said.

"People do not want to talk about *that*," Pat said.

And she's right.

It would pick the scab of the word "stress" and cause real blood to flow.

"So when my colleague asked me if my weight-loss was 'stress-related?' I said, 'Related' as cheerfully as I could."

She picked my scab and I bled quietly.

"Is daily conversation with people I see every day this meaningless?" I wondered.

"Yes," Brenda said. "That's why we're here."

"The literature on death is vast and profound," Macy said. "But I have not found anything that comforts me."

We are still wondering why Macy requires any comforting whatsoever, but she is such a valued presence in our group that we are in the strange position of not wanting to pry, especially since these are the first words Macy has uttered since her Hugh Michael share. *I am haunted by the fact that someone I had forgotten considered me so memorable.*

Macy recommended a change of venue for the group. Mike was all for it. Ann offered the basement of her church.

"I'm talking about a group trip out of the country," Macy said.

"Where to?" Brenda asked.

"Mexico. To celebrate The Day of the Dead."

"That's a laugh riot," Samantha said.

"No, seriously," Macy persisted. "What if we studied how people cope with death in other cultures?" There was a strained quality to her voice, as if she desperately needed to get out of town.

"We can certainly think about it," Brenda said. "The goal of this group is more therapeutic than academic," she explained. "In the meantime, we look forward to any cultural information you would like to share with us, Macy. We're lucky to have a librarian in the group."

Macy offered to come up with a reading list that might give us solace.

"Thank you for Pamuk's *Istanbul,*" I said.

"You're very welcome," Macy said, adding, "By the way, I just wanted to reassure you all that, even though I'm an atheist, I respect all your beliefs and I promise to include books rooted in them."

It strikes me that the farther away you are from death, the more thoroughly you enjoy and explore its literature. Like tourists researching a journey, inactive grievers want no surprises when they arrive at their final destination.

After a short coffee break, during which Pat finished her pack of Salems, Macy surprised us by doing all the talking.

"I lost a child," she began.

"I'm sorry," Brenda said.

"What!?" I whispered, rather hoarsely.

Brenda waved her hand to summon the group's attention. Though our bereavement counselor is equally sensitive to all members, she seemed particularly attuned to a tragedy she had experienced first-hand.

We were completely undone by this sudden and tragic admission. "I'm sorry," we all said in unison.

"How old was your child when she passed?"

"She would have been six."

"And how many years have you been harboring this grief?"

"Six," Macy said. Then she started to cry. Her Nefertiti eyeliner broke the banks of her huge dark eyes; tiny black rivulets ran down her cheek.

As if on cue, the rain tapped on the roof of the Nature Center. We all felt very sorry for Macy, for there is no worse loss. No loss more unnatural. No loss more profound. No loss more life changing. For a parent to lose a child.

I was so caught up in Macy's loss that I neglected to do the math. Brenda clearly had. "So *how* old was your child when he or she passed?"

"She was…she was…"

Jim handed her a tissue.

We were waiting now, because the rain was tapering off and we could all hear her quite clearly and Samantha, seated next to me, smelled as if Campbell's Cream of Tomato soup was coming out of her pores. Ann pursed her tiny features together; taken as a whole, they take up thirty percent of the fleshy circumference that constitutes her face. Mike yanked off his baseball cap, stroking the remaining gray hairs on his bald spot into guitar string formation. Jim rubbed his thumb over his newly buffed nails and Cheryl placed her hand on Macy's forearm. During this time, it was occurring to all of us that six minus six was zero and the tattoo of a baby on her upper arm was making more sense.

By now, the whole group was waiting.

"She was…"

"Zero!?" Brenda offered. Her hiking boot was tapping the air madly, until finally whatever had caused the tapping was flying out her mouth. "My daughter, Caroline, was hit by a school bus as I watched from the curb. Ann's son died of a head injury after hitting a tree in a snowboarding accident. Mike's daughter died of a heroin overdose. Jim's lover committed suicide when his HIV became AIDs. Samantha's husband was killed in Iraq. And you're here…" She turned to Macy. "Well, I don't *know* why *you're* here."

"I suffered a miscarriage," Macy said. "A little girl." She was barely audible. "I wanted to know."

"That's right, Macy," Brenda said mechanically, struggling to regain her composure, for she had been anything but pale lately. "We all need to validate your feelings."

"You don't sound sincere, Brenda," I said.

"I'm not," she said, quietly.

"I felt your irritation when Macy spoke of Hugh Michael," Jim said.

"Me too," Samantha said.

"Me three," Ann (Everything Happens for a Reason) Powell said. Her uncommonly robust voice matched her large, solid body.

"I can understand how you all got that impression," Brenda said.

It was tantamount to mutiny. We respected and cared about Brenda, but we were starting to question her ability to remain neutral.

"I think that Macy should find a group more suited to her needs."

Jim was obsessed with Macy's loss of Hugh Michael. Ann had bonded with Macy at the spa fundraiser. Mike thought Macy was as sexy as Joan Jett in her prime. Samantha thought it was unfair to exclude anybody who was suffering. Cheryl planned all her nephrology and cosmetic appointments around our bereavement group and did not want anyone to leave. Pat and I felt extremely protective of Macy.

Then the most unnerving thing happened. The very woman we looked up to as our group leader, with her sympathetic manner and her sweet soul minted by our common grief, the very Brenda we needed to be Brenda, was suddenly overcome with grief. She buried her face in her hands and wept.

Was she reliving her daughter's death? Reliving the agony of a loss she could not share? We sat transfixed, not knowing, reconstructing a scene she had seen first-hand and replayed in her mind thousands of times, every day, more so on holidays and especially on her daughter's birthday.

We sat in silence for the better part of the entire hour. Mike clasped his hands and lowered his head in silent prayer. One by one, we all did the same.

Finally, Brenda wiped her face with her hands and raised her head.

After another wave of rain, one sunburst, two thunderclaps, and a single rainbow, Brenda said, "I'm sorry, Macy. Please continue."

Macy's voice was drained. "My husband was devastated. We have not been able to conceive since my miscarriage."

"Oh, Macy. I'm so sorry," I said, turning toward her. Whatever difficulties I have endured, I cannot imagine my life without Sam and Grace.

STICKY MATS

Six days after our Oregon shore adventure, Lucas brought our fitness regime inside. He invited Pat and Bill to a free body-fat evaluation in the Bod Pod, along with the *least* EXTREME class our club has to offer.

While Bill and Lucas dropped the children in Kids Club, I drove Pat, alone, because we never have time to talk. We hadn't fully discussed Macy's bombshell share after our last meeting. We were also long overdue for our elephant-in-the-room, come-to-Jesus, camel's-nose-in-the-tent, take-me-to-church conversation about Lucas and Bill. But *Why not begin with Macy?*

"What did you make of Macy's story?" I asked.

"I love Macy, but we've all had miscarriages."

I had not and Pat knew that. I knew that she *had* miscarried, so I avoided that topic altogether.

"Brenda wasn't exactly easy on Macy," Pat said.

"True. But I think it brought us all closer. We cleared the air."

"Speaking of which," Pat said, as if ticking another routine item off her to-do list, "Bill likes you."

I opened my mouth, but nothing came out, so I shut it again.

Unsure of what Pat meant by *like*, I replied as honestly as I could. "I like him too. He's a good man."

"Yes, he is."

"Lucas likes you too."

"But not in the way that Bill likes you."

"*I would never even consider –*" I pronounced forcefully and evenly.

"I know. He wouldn't either. You two are the most trustworthy people I know. Which is why I can tell you the truth. We're not doing so well."

She pulled out a cigarette and lit it.

Sounds and images surged out of nowhere: *oxygen tanks, tubes, coughing, radiation, the withering away...*

"I *know*! I promised Bill I'd quit." She turned toward me, staring at my hands. "Are you okay?"

My thumbs were tapping the steering wheel the way my father's used to when he needed a nicotine fix.

"We used to have lots of fun," Pat resumed, "but we've started bickering like a sexless old couple and this was supposed to be a fun visit."

My emotions were so confused and conflicted that I burst into tears.

"WHAT THE FUCK, JULIETTE!?"

I could not stop.

Pat was frantic. "Want me to drive!?"

Big blubbering tears. Foggy vision. I pulled over and buried my face in the steering wheel. I felt Pat's hand rubbing my heaving back, which only made things worse.

After a few minutes, Alicia Keys's "Empire State of Mind" ringtone jarred the stillness.

"Juliette," Pat said, silencing her phone. "Look at me."

I lifted my head and turned toward her.

"You're scaring me," she said. "You need to tell me what's bothering you."

"Bill's right."

"About *what?*"

I was so drained that I stared at her cigarette with a frozen calmness. "I want you to quit. If anything happens to you, I'm not sure I can endure another loss."

"What are you talking about?" she asked gently. "I'm here right now. I promise I'll visit more often, and *nothing* is going to happen to me!"

"I don't want you to die the way my father did."

"Oh for *chrissakes!*" she yelled. "Is *that* all you're worried about? I'm not going to die!"

"That's what my father said!"

"Even if I do, Stage 4 would be after I was dead anyway."

"That's *exactly* what my father said!"

"I loved your father!" She burst into tears.

"So did I!"

"You know what?" she shouted, grabbing her Salem Lights and waving them furiously in front of my face. "I've HAD it!" With the back of her sleeve, she wiped the waterworks from her eyes and nose, yanked the door open, and marched angrily towards the Chuck E. Cheese on the corner. She turned back towards me, waving the Salems like a metronome on its fastest setting, then punched them down the gullet of a trash bin. "I FUCKING QUIT! HERE AND NOW! I FUCKING *FUCKING* QUIT!"

My eyes started flooding again.

She stormed back to my Fiesta, opened the door, sat down, and took a deep breath. "I wouldn't do this for Bill, but I'll quit smoking for you."

I mopped my face with the tissues on my car visor.

"I have two conditions," she said.

"What are they?"

"Stop crying."

"Okay," I snort-sniffled, took a deep breath, and sat up with resolve.

"And before we get to the club, you'll need to buy me some Nicorette."

Lucas met us in front of the Kids Club. "Are you guys okay?"

"We're fine," I said.

"Why do you ask?" Pat replied coolly.

He laughed. "Because you both look like raspberries, all red and puffy."

"We're worried about someone in our bereavement group," Pat said somberly.

I wondered what she'd throw out next. "How are the kids?" I asked.

"Great! Kids Club has art, basketball, and rock climbing today."

"And for the adults?" I asked.

"There's a new class I think you might like. Not so sure about Pat. It's a fusion of yoga, Pilates, and t'ai chi."

Lucas tells me the class will offset the foggy, wet gloom that's drowning the "happy" chemicals in my head. He draws my brain on the back of the Kids Club schedule. "This is Juliette's brain before exercise," he says. After exercise, (he grabs the Crayola neons), your pleasure centers are lit up like the Wheel of Fortune slots in Vegas.

Pat smiled. "Will my brain look like that too?"

As a man of science, Lucas acknowledges that the teacher's claims are hazier. For Valinda, the Yoga Flow instructor, every pose involves a release of toxins from one or more major organ. When my father was ill, I walked out of a Bikram class when the teacher asked us to raise our hands if we had cancer. One poor man waved in response, after which the teacher declared cheerfully, "No more cancer with this pose!"

We agreed that the free body-fat screening should be done before lunch, though Pat and I are more interested in two other special events. A Chi Master is giving free chi readings and tonight there's a wine tasting hosted by Oregon's latest wine industry import from France, oenologist and sommelier Jean-Claude Gaulois.

While Jean-Claude Gaulois was setting up for his wine tasting in the club's lobby, dozens of club members lined up next to the climbing wall to have their body fat tested. The technician explained how it works, which goes something like this: Instead of displacement of water by volume (Archimedes), they're displacing air. Somehow the machine knows how much air and, by increasing the pressure, they get a magic reading of a person's body fat, internal and external. More accurate than calipers, the technician insists.

For the most accurate reading, the Bod Pod technician told everyone to wear form-fitting clothes, including a swim cap.

Twenty minutes later, Pat emerged from the women's locker room wearing spandex from head to toe.

The technician lifted the bubble lid and Pat stepped in. He lowered the dome and told Pat to hold her breath, on his count, for a few seconds.

After five minutes, the results were in.

"May I share the results?" the technician asked.

"I insist," Pat said.

"Level of fat sometimes found in *elite athletes*," the technician said, reading from his chart.

Pat waved, acknowledging the murmurs of admiration from the gathering crowd.

"Impossible," Carol said, emerging from the end of the line. She was wearing a spandex unitard in colors rivaling those of a tropical bird.

"What are you saying?" Mr. Bod Pod asked.

"She's in good shape, but she's a smoker."

"They're not doing a PET Scan, Carol," Lucas muttered under his breath.

Pat ripped off her swim cap. Glossy auburn curls cascaded down her back. Gaulois looked up. *"Elle est belle, cette femme,"* he said aloud, as if voicing his pleasure for a complex Chateau Croix Mouton Prize Bordeaux.

"Why don't you get in that spaceship, Carol?" Bill said, in solidarity with Pat. "We'll see what your results look like."

Pat was enjoying her 15 minutes of fame.

"High-five, sister!" one ironwoman smiled.

Pat responded by raising the glass Gaulois had just slipped her, a three-ounce pour of Pinot Gris.

I wound my way from the back of the crowd and stood behind Carol and hissed, "What *is* your problem!?"

"You are," she said.

"Fine," I said, knowing that nothing was fine. "Leave Pat out of it."

"Mia told me *all about* you and Pat!" she taunted. "And how *dare* you go camping with my children?"

Bill's timing was perfect. "Your turn, Carol."

"No, it's not."

Lucas walked over, picked Carol up, and dropped her in the spot Bill had vacated on her behalf.

"Take it easy, dude," a rock climber called down from his perch. They are very quick to pick up on hostility in Oregon. He pushed off an ear on a massive climbing wall pegged with thousands of jujubee noses, feet, and fanciful shapes. Then he belayed own.

"We all have something to learn from Pat," the Bod Pod man said. "So *don't get testy,*" he said to Carol.

The rock climber began nudging Lucas towards the plastic bubble chanting, "*Bod in pod!*" And the club members joined in, "*Bod in pod!*"

"I'll go in, if you get back in line," Lucas said to Bill.

"Deal." Bill saw me trying to edge out of view. "You too, Juliette."

"I can't!" I said, scanning the room, appealing to Jean-Claude Gaulois to take my place. *Absolument pas.* His glance said, "*Non!*"

Carol Vesuvius Spandexi Tropicalus headed towards me the second she emerged from the Bod Pod.

"I'm ready!" I cried.

Lucas's Bod Pod results came in as Lean. "You look ridiculous in spandex," Carol sniped. Bill's results came in as Lean, beating Lucas by one percent. In jest, Lucas demanded a rematch, then shook Bill's hand. Carol was Moderately Lean (23-30%).

"She's one of those skinny fat people my doctor warns me I'll become," Pat said.

To my shock, I came in as Ultra-Lean and the crowd clapped. *So this is sports.* For the first time in my life, I'd won a competition.

The climbing wall pacifist, along with dozens of club members and trainers, nudged me towards Gaulois's wine display, where he handed me a coupe of champagne. My thrill of victory. Carol's agony of defeat. Next year, with proper training, Pat and I will be off to the strongest women in the world contest, live on ESPN from Kuala Lumpur.

Instead of the Yoga Fusion class Lucas recommended, Pat elected to take a spin class. Bill decided to take Valinda's class with me.

He unrolled his purple sticky mat next to mine and smiled.

"I thought I'd give it a go," he said. "Pat's spinning with Lucas."

He got me a block and a strap.

"Thanks."

"My pleasure."

To his credit, Bill is the only person without a water bottle. Don't get me started on water bottles. Yoginis pop the caps of their liter bottles and take a swig. Sometimes they swig as often as every third pose. If I were a water molecule, I would be irritated by the gratuitous displacement. This is not Death Valley. This is not the Sahara. They cap and uncap the giver-of-life, gulping and drenching themselves to punctuate their minimal exertions between poses. And don't get me started on the breathing. The least inhibited men and women inhale and grunt as if they're having sex.

Maybe it's my (fallen) Catholic roots. We're a quiet bunch. I have vague memories of mass in Latin. *In nomine Patris, et Filii, et Spiritus Sancti.*

There is something to be said for restraint.

"Lucas is a very determined fellow," Bill said. "You've got to admire that."

"I do."

Even if Bill is sincere about Lucas, which he might be, the only way to deal with someone curious about your personal life is to change the subject. I asked Bill about the conference that took him away from our campsite and literally left us in a tangle. Pat's airborne sea animals ended up in a pile of kite string, which took us two hours to unravel.

"I'm so sorry," he said, crossing his legs. "But the conference really was outstanding."

I retrieved a lavender eye pillow from the wicker basket in the back of the room and handed it to him.

"Thanks." He smiled.

"My pleasure." I rolled onto my back.

"Juliette?"

"What?"

"I'm thinking about accepting a job in Los Angeles."

"What kind of job?"

"Port of Los Angeles and more airport security."

Valinda came in and lowered the lights.

"We can talk about your job over lunch," I whispered. "Lucas invited us."

Valinda asks us to take slow, deep breaths to start. I am having trouble doing this.

Bill does very well. He is so attentive that Valinda is constantly coming over to correct his practice, and he whispers, "Thank you," which she finds charming, despite her cool-cat yogini aura.

Valinda guides us through the relaxation period. She turns off the lights and takes us on a journey, up and down the chakras. Today, she added a new chakra, which she had never mentioned before Bill's attendance. "Red chakra. Male sexual energy." From the corner of my eye, I saw Bill pop his eyes open and smile.

During shavasana I always put a towel over my eyes. I think of those I've lost when I'm supposed to be breathing and quieting my chattering mind. Too many people I love are not breathing and will never breathe again.

Yet something very odd is happening today. I am stretching and lying back in the dark and it's hot and my muscles are warm and my body is open and, for once, for one blessed moment, rather than releasing some clenched fist of pain in my mind, I am feeling, all-too-graphically, a man making love to me. I am surrendering to the purest of impure thoughts from the most instinctive root of primal desire.

Until the woman behind me started to cry and ruined it all.

After we had said our *namastes*, I turned my head and, thinking I should cheer up a newcomer to the class, I whispered, "Are you okay?"

"I just feel like crying," she said. She lay in the dark, still in corpse pose, wrapped in her blanket like a mummy, her voice smothered by the towel over her head.

"Yoga can release a lot of emotions," I said gently.

After Valinda flicked on the lights, the woman removed her towel, then her eye pillow. Carol Schell, Lucas's ex-wife-to-be, was Vesuvius recumbent.

Bill looked over as if to say, *yikes,* and rolled up his mat. Then he picked up his block, his strap, and glided between us, returning his equipment to the bins in the back of the room.

"FYI," he whispered, as I lay my mat in the bin, "she's crying because Lucas is obsessed with you."

"Tell her there's nothing between us."

"I can't say that."

"Why?"

"Because I saw him outside the yurt covering his manhood with a frying pan."

"*Unconsummated*, thanks to you," I said. "So you *can* tell her."

153

By the time I returned my block, Valinda was welcoming Carol to our yoga class. To release her pain, Valinda recommended that Carol try a new African dance class, with live drums, and make an appointment with today's visiting Chi Master.

I found Lucas waiting for me by the water fountain, looking a bit standoffish. He didn't have his habitual ravenous look–as if he expected me to throw my arms around him, drop my knickers, fetch a mat, and mount him in the squash court.

"I didn't want to bring this up in front of Kids Club with Pat," he said, "but Grace told me everything, and I just wanted to tell you that I'm still processing it."

"Processing *what?*"

"I'm not supposed to know, and Grace does not want to get in trouble."

"I'm her mother."

"I know. But she said you wanted to keep it a secret."

"Keep *what* a secret?"

"Maybe you should talk to her after lunch."

Then he pulled me into the squash court and turned off the lights.

Lucas had invited Bill, Pat, and me to lunch; but first he wanted us to meet Carl Fortuna, the elderly man Lucas had volunteered to film. Carl is determined to train and compete in a cycling race while battling cancer. I admire Lucas for his compassion. I had agreed to lunch, but at that moment I was feeling vulnerable and reminded myself that Lucas was separated, but not formally divorced. Moreover, though I do not feel connected to Lake Oswego, I am perceived as a member of the community. My children attend the same school as Mia and Joey. They play on the same soccer fields. They take books (okay, movies) out of the same library. I do not want to get kicked out of another book club, as I had back East in Larchmont, especially if my behavior affects my children's social status. I feel like any native of a foreign country who wants his or her children to assimilate. For their sake, I do not want to make waves, rock the boat, or upset any proverbial apple cart. Above all, I do not want anyone to think that I am some marriage-wrecking, hoochie-mama, naughty elementary schoolteacher. Close encounters with Our Lady of the Lava are inevitable: Sam and Joey play together. After Poetry Day, Mia became Grace's best friend.

The door to the squash court opened and I was blinded by light. I felt a firm hand on my shoulder.

"We'll wait for you guys by the restaurant," Bill said. "What's the name of the cyclist you want us to meet?"

"Carl Fortuna," Lucas said. "He's waiting near the climbing wall, next to the Bod Pod."

As Bill turned to leave, my eyes followed him, beginning their peripheral scan for Carol.

Lucas smiled. "She's not here."

"It's not funny! I feel like she's stalking me. *She's everywhere.*"

His stare was so intense that his mood-ring green

eyes made retinal prints when I looked away.

"You need to slow down," I said.

"I will." He moved closer. He was one breath away, his lips within striking distance. He turned off the lights and kissed me, full smash and lingering.

"They're waiting for us," I whispered. I reached for his hands and held them. "Are you sure there's no hope for you and Carol?"

"Yes." He pressed his forehead against mine and would not look up until I asked, "What's the matter?"

"I just hope there's hope for us."

The light flicked on. Bill opened the glass door. "Are you finished with your squash game?" He glanced at Lucas as if he were a national security threat.

"Yes," I said.

"Carl is looking for Lucas."

"Be right there," Lucas said.

When it was clear that Bill would not move, Lucas went on ahead, leaving me to deal with Bill behaving like the Reverend Dimmesdale in Hawthorne's *Scarlet Letter*.

As we made our way to the lobby, I was so mad at Bill that I smacked him in the sternum. "I can take care of myself," I said.

"I'm not convinced," he said.

I would have hit him again, but my knuckles ached. Bill's abs were as taut as a bongo.

"My life is none of your business."

Bill stopped walking. "You've made it my business. Pat's your best friend and I just told Carol there was nothing between you and her husband."

"You did?"

"Yes."

"Thank you."

"So which is it?"

"Which is what?"

"What's going on with you and Lucas?"

"We're figuring things out."

"You're fragile," Bill said. "Pat says it. I see it."

"What's going on with you and Pat?" I asked, with a retaliatory strike that was unlike me.

"Maybe you should ask Pat."

I did not tell him that Pat had already confided their troubles to me. I wanted to scream with joy that my best friend was giving up smoking. I never would have added, *for me*, because it doesn't matter. Or maybe it does with regard to *their* relationship.

Lucas, Pat, and Carl watched us approach from the opposite end of the club's long grey industrial carpet interspersed with yellow and red squares. Our walk took me back to the day Bill or "Bob," so I'd thought, brought us to our gate at the Los Angeles airport.

"Did you know that I was Pat's Juliette the day I met you?"

"No."

"Didn't you check my ID?"

He raised his eyebrows, as if to underscore the implied insult.

"When did you find out?"

"The same day you did."

Carl Fortuna, the subject of Lucas's documentary, was a wiry man in his early sixties who hailed Lucas and hugged him with the intensity reserved for Pearl Harbor veterans or survivors of major disasters.

"I want you to meet some friends of mine," Lucas said.

Carl was so thin I could see every vein in his arm. "You must be Juliette," he said, gripping my hand as if it were the last one he would ever hold.

A few weeks after Lucas met Carl, his doctors found cancer at the base of his sacrum. The cancer was a sarcoma that metastasized to his lungs. The surgeons removed one of his lungs and left thirty more tumors in his remaining lung. Despite this, Carl completed a "Reach the Beach" 103-mile charity ride for the American Lung Association.

"I'd like to donate," I told Carl.

"We would too," Pat said.

Lucas looked pleasantly surprised and thanked us for our support. "I'm documenting Carl's quest to participate in Cycle Portland. It's a 400-mile course, over six days, including a 5000-foot vertical gain over a distance of 40 miles. The finish line is at Crater Lake."

Lucas has written letters to various television stations; he wants to air the film on ESPN's *American Heroes* and share Carl's story on the talk show circuit. A friend from Nike promises to handle the marketing.

"Are you up for this, Carl?" Bill asked.

"When I'm on my bike, I feel alive," he said. "It's that simple."

Over lunch, Lucas waxed forth about the upcoming Oregon Mud Festival. Lucas is reading *The Clay Cure*.

"The author, Ran Knishinsky, has been eating dirt every day for the past six years," Lucas said. "Over 200 cultures worldwide drink clay every day."

"Do they serve clay here?" Pat asked in a droll, flat voice as the hostess handed us menus.

"Not yet," Lucas smiled. "But I found a website where they sell Pascalite. It's a bit different, but a form of calcium bentonite called Montmorillonite. It was named after the French-Canadian trapper and prospector, Emile Pascal."

"Are you ready to order?" the server asked.

"Not yet," Bill said. "We're mired in mud."

"Not to put too fine a point on it, but clay is actually very different from mud," Lucas said.

I laughed. Lucas was trying to vex the out-of-towners with an Oregonian information dump.

The server doubled as the Kids Club's climbing wall instructor. She smiled and asked how Sam and Grace were doing. "I love your kids," she said. I fist pounded my heart in a back-at-you gesture as Lucas droned on.

"After mining clay in the Big Horn Mountains, Pascal applied the cream-colored mud to his badly chapped hands and sunburned nose and was amazed by its healing powers," Lucas said. "Pascalite's used in soap and toothpaste. It's applied as a poultice to insect bites, sunburns, infections, cold sores, and acne, and as a suppository for hemorrhoids."

"Lucas, we're having lunch," Bill said.

"Shoot me now," Pat said.

"Sounds like something useful for camping," I said, smiling to myself. Bill nudged me under the table with his foot; his eyes said, don't encourage him.

"Exactly," Lucas said. "It's used for skin cleaning and conditioning–for heartburn, for ulcers—and as a natural mineral and dietary supplement. Ranchers and veterinarians have used it for wounds and infections on livestock."

"Let's talk about moss," Bill said.

"My lawn has a *serious* moss problem," I said, avoiding Bill's reaction. "I have Rhytidiaedelpus where I want it and Brachythecium albicans where I don't want it."

"I'm glad you asked about moss," Lucas smiled, winking at me in solidarity. "Moss is a subject I know something about."

I started to laugh. I could not stop.

"Oh Christ!" Pat moaned. "Stop laughing, Juliette. It only goads him on."

"Pat," Lucas said, taking it to the next level. "Are you aware that Oregon sheet moss is a great cage substrate for amphibians and wetland environment reptiles? It works great in egg-laying chambers."

A full laugh-burst propelled a fizzy burst of Coke Zero inside my nose.

"Juliette, what's gotten into you?" Pat asked. Despite her annoyance, I sensed she was happy to see me happy.

I wanted to shout *Pat quit smoking*, but the news was so precious and so recent, I treasured the confidence.

Lucas smiled broadly. "I love the sound of Juliette's laughter," he said. Just as he was reaching for my hand, Bill hiked his elbow on the table and challenged Lucas to an arm wrestle.

"Sure," Lucas said, grabbing Bill's hand. "No cheating."

"What is it with you two!?" Pat smiled, shaking her head.

"Healthy male rivalry," Bill said.

"I'm still smarting from my Bod Pod defeat," Lucas said.

"You're worse than children," I said, trying to appear ladylike as I wiped soda from my nose with a paper napkin.

In the midst of wrestling Lucas, Bill startled me by offering his hand for a simultaneous thumb war. "One, two, three, four, I declare an act of war. Five, six, seven, eight, you're the thumb I really hate."

All my thumb-wrestling with Sam and Gracie was paying off; I beat Bill easily. "Rematch," I offered, clasping his strong, warm hand.

He and Lucas were really going at it.

"Let's talk about your work," Lucas said.

"Stop trying to distract me."

"Will you two idiots stop?" Pat said. "You're an embarrassment."

They ignored her.

"Okay. Pat," Lucas said, "let's talk about you and Juliette."

We ignored them.

Lucas prevailed over Bill; then Bill reversed Lucas's lead. With astonishing power and determination, Lucas reversed the near win, with Bill's hand hovering two inches off the table.

"Time out," the server said, smiling as she handed me napkins. She placed another Coke Zero in front of me and put three iced teas in the line of fire. "If you knock these over, you'll all have to change back into your Spandex," she said. Minutes later, she returned with three burgers and Lucas's tofu special.

"It's a tie," Pat said, taking a bite out of her burger to signal an end to the arm wrestle.

"Bill's right," Lucas conceded. "Enough about moss, let's talk about his work."

"Before you talk about work, Bill," I said, "I'd like to resolve this moss issue once and for all."

"God no," Pat said, dipping a French fry into ketchup.

I explained to Bill and Lucas that I had researched the matter in the Lewis and Clark library. According to studies conducted by Oregon State University, crypto-cidal soap is the most humane way for moss to die. "Think of it as assisted suicide for moss," I said.

"Did I just hear you say assisted suicide for moss?" Bill asked.

I nodded.

"Juliette's lost her mind," Pat said.

Lucas smiled.

Bill started laughing, softly at first; then he completely lost control. He excused himself from the table. When he returned, he caught my eye; another outburst ricocheted from him to me and redoubled its force with a vengeance. It reminded me of all the times we caught my mother cheating at Scrabble. Crazy laugh, the French call it.

When Lucas first showed an interest in me, I felt a surge of resistance. An emotional house of cards that was followed by the sudden, internal thump of an edifice crashing, the wreckage of which forced me to ask myself what I was doing with my life or wasting time with people I did not connect with. During lunch, I did not feel that way. To my surprise, Lucas had a sense of humor.

Lucas atoned for his mud lecture by picking up the check. Bill and Pat thanked him but declined his invitation to attend the Oregon Mud Festival.

"I'll take the kids," he said, smiling at me. "They'll love it."

Years of yoga and meditation did not stop my chattering mind from wondering what Mia had told her mother; nor did it suppress my questions about Lucas's earlier comment about Grace's right to privacy.

I wanted to pull Sam and Grace out of Kids Club to interrogate Grace, but Lucas had already signed us up for the visiting Chi Master. According to Valinda, Chi Master can diagnose problems regarding the life force and spirit present in all things. He can also recalibrate your chi if it's off-balance. When things are really off-kilter, he approaches people as if they are a biohazard.

"Spicy," he said. The Chi Master approached me with latex gloves. "Your chi is spicy."

"That means you're angry," Lucas whispered.

I asked Lucas to wait for me outside.

"Angry," the Chi Master explained, after Lucas left. I was eating too many spicy things, so I was angry.

"My parents died," I explained.

He insisted that the anger was not from my parents.

"You must release the anger," he said.

"How?"

"Identify the source and strike at its heart."

"Violence!?"

"No. There are many ways to strike."

"Like what?"

"You will find the first strike very soon, then the next, and unblock the anger."

Pat was next. "You are from the East Coast," he smiled. "Big energy. Complicated chi."

"I'm trying to quit smoking. Is that why?"

"Maybe one reason. Try tai chi class for relaxation."

Jean-Claude Gaulois entered. While we were at lunch, Gaulois had finished setting up his wine tasting table.

"I study grapes. I am an oenologist," he told the Chi Master. When the Chi Master asked if Gaulois wanted privacy, he said, "They are my new friends. My only friends. They can stay."

In the course of his convoluted explanation, it became clear that Jean-Claude's mistress really was the Dijon clone. He claims that the chardonnays of the Willamette Valley are fine enough to compete with those of *La Bourgogne* (Burgundy), but he was hired to cultivate pinot grapes. He has great admiration for Oregon's pinots, but he believes that the Oregon chardonnay bears watching, as it contains far less oak than its California rival, which he calls, *"du parfum."* He patted his body as if applying cologne.

Before moving to America, Gaulois read a seminal book, which he said changed his life. From *What Color is Your Parachute?*, Gaulois learned that his life's work involved animals, children, and grapes.

"I am lonely, *bien sur*, but I feel more at home," he said.

The Chi Master was concerned about Gaulois. "Most spicy," he said. He gave Gaulois some breathing exercises and asked him to return in one week.

Bill went last. I detected a look of sympathy when the Chi Master looked at him.

"You have suffered in the past. Now there is harmony."

On the way to the kids club, we said goodbye to Carl, who was the last club member waiting for his Bod Pod consultation. I didn't know how to say it to Lucas, but it's obvious that this poor, sweet man standing patiently in line is dying. His face is gaunt, his body desiccated, with bruises the color of eggplants.

Lucas does not see it. He wants what Carl wants, but I wonder if Lucas's positive thinking borders on the grotesque. As for Carl, is he pushing himself beyond the bounds of human decency, dignity, and endurance?

Bill approached Carl. "I'm pretty fit and I can't possibly do what you're doing. Are you sure you're up for Cycle Portland?"

"Yes," he said. "Otherwise, I wouldn't be doing it."

As for Pat, I could read her mind: *Everybody's dying.*

Later, when the sun streamed through our club window, I remembered how my father missed Daylight Savings by a week. He could not venture outside from October until he died. Instead, he chose to be with my mother on her birthday. It was stoic of him to endure a particularly difficult New England winter. He loved the spring and it breaks my heart that he missed it.

My father held on until my mother's birthday; then let go, precisely.

Letter to the Afterlife

Dear Mom,
Today, I got an attack of the *fou rire*, which is wonderfully contagious. It reminded me of your crazy laugh during Scrabble games, after Dad, who memorized Scrabble's letter distribution list, identified missing s's and one q's only to find that you were stockpiling letters in your pocket.

Shame on you!

Love,
Juliette

Letter to the Afterlife

Dear Dad,
You told Pat never to start, but short of that, you will be ELATED to know that today PAT QUIT SMOKING!!!!!!!!!

Thanks to the molten anger reading from our health club's Chi Master, I am sending a letter

excoriating the judge who ruled in Nick's favor
when he was unhinged.

Love,
Juliette

Letter to The Supreme Court of the State of New York

Dear Justice Jamison,

The Chi Master at my health club has put his
finger on what I believe to be one source of my
latent anger.

You will not remember me, but you are the judge
who declared me a flight risk and awarded 100%
primary custody to an absentee workaholic
father with an adult onset of psychopathy.

How massively your ten minutes in court
changed our lives forever.

No wonder my chi is "spicy."

With all due respect,
Fuck You.

Juliette

P.S. My children, Sam and Grace, are okay, no
thanks to you.

TEACH YOUR CHILDREN WELL II

After a full day at the health club, I was grateful when Grandma and Grandpa offered to cook chicken tikka masala and saag paneer for dinner. As I passed the naan, I re-calculated which guest would get the sofa, Aerobed, or full queen: Sam's birthday + 8; Mother's Day + 32; and/or Memorial Day + 10 inter- mittent/4 actual? When dinner was over, I finished my lesson plan and called Lucas at his new apartment in order to coax out background material for my conver- sation with Grace. He restated his position, protecting her as if she were a legal client, then said something very odd.

"Maybe you *shouldn't* talk to her. I might be okay with what Grace said."

"I don't know what she said. And I don't know what Carol was talking about in reference to Mia."

"Carol knows we went camping."

"As she should. A mother should always know where her children are."

"She's driving me nuts."

"This is just the beginning. Is that why you were a bit reserved today?"

"I'm scared, Juliette."

"Why?"

"Because I love Joey and Mia and the little you've told me about your custody battle is horrifying. You're stronger than I am."

"What's the alternative?"

"Living hell."

I scanned my bookcase during the ensuing silence. When my eyes landed on *Macbeth*, I wanted to say, "Screw your courage to the sticking-place," but uttered the far less blood-thirsty and more practical, "I've got beds to make tonight and tomorrow I'm teaching my fourth graders about puberty."

Lucas laughed softly.

From the family room, the entire intro to *Bill Nye the Science Guy* elapsed before I changed course with a compliment. "You are an accomplished kisser."

Still no reply.

I was about to abandon what felt like an exorcism when Lucas said, "I know about you and Pat."

"You know *what* about me and Pat?"

"That you have feelings for her."

"Of course I do. She's my best friend."

"Feelings that go beyond friendship."

As a teacher, I do my best to give my fourth graders sensitive, factual, age-appropriate societal tools to talk about sex and gender. As a parent, I often leave the subject to the schools. Oregon is extremely progressive in this regard and I *cannot wait* until Grace takes Sex Ed with Miss Bundy next year. In our family, the sex ed thing has gone too far and, unlike my students, my children have turned the societal tools entrusted to them against their mother.

I pulled Grace into the den.

"You said we could watch *Bill Nye* with everybody."

"I did, but I need to talk to you."

"Can we talk after the show?"

"No. What did you tell Lucas when we went camping?"

"I already told you," she said, shifting her gaze toward the bookcase. "Mia misses her mom."

"What else did you say to Lucas?"

She sighed. "The other part is private."

"Did you say something about me?"

"Yes."

"Then it's not private. I'm your mother."

"I told him you were a lesbian."

"Do you know what a lesbian is?"

"Yes."

"What?"

"It's a woman who loves women."

"So if you love Mia, does that make you a lesbian?"

"I don't think so."

"Well, I'm not a lesbian."

"It's okay to be gay, Mom!"

"Of course it is, but I'm not gay."

"Where are you getting this information?"

"Sam and Joey are studying this stuff in Miss Bundy's class."

"But why would you even bring it up with Mr. Schell?" When she was silent, I persisted. "Why would you tell him something I think you know is not true?"

She looked frantic. "SAM!"

When he did not respond, I pulled him into the den.

"I want to watch *Bill Nye*! Can I ask them to pause it?"

I nodded. When Sam returned, a suspicious look passed between him and Grace, as if they were pacing and eyeing each other before a duel.

"What's going on?" he asked.

"I *didn't* tell her what you told Mr. Schell," Grace said.

"What did I tell Mr. Schell!?"

"The sex ed stuff."

"Sam, what did you tell Lucas?" I asked.

"I said I thought you were cisgender."

"What's that?" Grace asked.

"It means that Mom is okay with the sex she was born with."

"So you think I'm cisgender and Grace thinks I'm a lesbian."

"Joey says you can be both. Grace is *never* factual."

"Why were you both discussing *any* of this with Mr. Schell?"

"I don't know," Sam cried. "Ask Grace. She started it."

"Did you tell anyone else I was a lesbian?"

"I thought you said you were *not*!" Grace said.

"I'm not. I'm asking you if you told anyone else."

Grace started to cry. "Only Mia."

This explains the game of telephone, with a direct line to the mouth of Vesuvius.

"Why did you bring up *any* of this, Grace Jeanne Louise Kristina Gayen?"

Grace knows I'm angry when I pronounce all nine syllables of her name. She wiped her eyes with one sleeve, her nose with the other, and yelled, "Because Mia misses her mother and you're spending too much time with Mr. Schell!"

I prayed that Pat, Bill, and the grandparents had not heard her. "We're spending time with *all of you*!" I did not refer to the Jamba Juice Agreement.

"Is that why you chimed in, Sam?"

"No! Joey and I were just saying stuff Miss Bundy is teaching us in class."

"Joey, you can finish *Bill Nye*. I need to talk to Grace in private."

"I'm sorry, Mom," she sniveled.

"You need to understand that these lessons are very important for reasons you just learned."

She nodded, looking down at her bunny slippers.

"If you think I don't spend enough time with you, you need to tell me."

She nodded again.

"You may *not* tell a story that is false and affects other people to get what you want. That will always backfire."

She did not nod.

"Grace Jeanne Louise Kristina Gayen!"

She looked up.

"Do you understand?"

"Yes," she whispered.

"Finally," I said. "Are we clear that a tampon is not a Band-Aid you stick up your vagina?"

"Yes."

"Are we clear that you *can* use a tampon and still be a virgin?"

"Yes."

"And what's a virgin?"

"Someone from Virginia."

Five minutes later, Sam dropped in, looking extremely uncomfortable.

"What's wrong?"

"You say you're not a lesbian, but do you like men?"

"Of course. Why?"

He drummed the fingers of his right hand against his pant leg, his signature sign of nerves. "Did you like Dad?"

Letter to the Afterlife

Dear Mom and Dad,

You are both very lucky that sex ed was in its primitive phases in my elementary school. I graduated with A's in all my biology classes without knowing that a snake had a penis (still hard to believe, actually).

These days, seaweed has a sex life and gender is fluid—*very* difficult concepts to explain to my students and especially to Sam and Grace.

I'm having enough trouble *avoiding* the reasons why Pat gets the sofa, Bill gets the Aerobed, and Grandma and Grandpa get the queen.

Thanks to the disinformation disseminated by your granddaughter, my suitor thinks I'm bisexual, his wife is convinced I'm a lesbian, my son thinks I hate men, and my daughter thinks the entire state of Virginia is inhabited by virgins.

All my love,
Juliette

15

BEREAVERS IV

P at was playing the new fidget app on her phone on the way to the Nature Center. I assumed it was because she had reached her maximum dose of Nicorette, which, as it turns out, is a very poor substitute for Salem Lights.

"This is my last bereavement group," she said.

"I thought you had one more Wednesday!"

"No. I fly out the Tuesday after Father's Day."

She sounded tense and I *hated* the idea of her leaving Oregon. Thanks to Pat and the group, I had finally begun to feel *consistently* better.

Until she dropped an atomic bomb, which poisoned my psyche and stripped my nerve endings bare.

Pat's hand shot up as soon as Brenda convened the group.

"I came to Oregon after recommending this group for Juliette. But I wanted to be surrounded by grief-stricken people when I told Juliette something I could not tell her at the time."

"Told me what?"

Pat froze.

"Told her what?" Brenda asked.

"Two years ago, Juliette called me. I had never heard her so anxious. She asked me to pick up Sam and Grace because her parent-teacher conferences were running late. Nick was making her crazy. He'd stopped working so he wouldn't have to pay any support. He told the court she was a flight risk and got 100 percent custody. She fought and won, but he was crazed. He filed for 100 percent custody a second time when Juliette was 15 minutes late on the court-ordered day of transfer."

My heart was racing, and I felt very sick.

"Sam and Grace were so happy so see me. They were eight and seven and were begging to see their puppy."

Brenda asked me if I was okay and I must have nodded.

"I was right on time. Nick was in the second-floor window of their brownstone, waiting for Sam and Grace. He was tall, handsome, perfectly dressed, and completely expressionless. When he didn't return Sam and Grace's waves, I made a snap decision."

Mike ran for a trash basket and stuck it in front of my chair.

"I grabbed their hands, did an about face, and hurried towards Broadway. The kids were confused. *Where are we going!? We want to see the puppy!*"

And here Pat broke down.

"Five blocks later, I heard an explosion."

"You had no idea the explosion was related to Nick?" Jim asked.

"No. I was simply terrified that Juliette would lose custody."

"You did the right thing," Cheryl said firmly.

"Not legally," Pat mumbled.

"*Fuck Legally!*" Mike yelled.

"*Thank God!*" Macy cried. She stood up, pacing with increasing agitation, unaware she was knocking over nests and other Nature Center displays.

"For Chrissakes, they could be dead!" Samantha said.

Ann's hands were clasped in prayer.

"Pat," Brenda asked, "do you believe Nick intended for Sam and Grace to be in the townhouse when he blew it up?"

"I know you all think I've judged Nick harshly, but it's because there's a huge difference between taking your own life and taking the lives of innocent children with you. It's the difference between suicide and murder. So the answer to your question is, yes. There is absolutely no question in my mind."

I threw up so violently I do not remember anything after that.

16

FATHER'S DAY

Two years ago, I stood at the scene of a howling absence, avoiding anyone besides my closest friends and family, as well as investigators assigned to the case. For a solid week, the tabloids and divorce lawyers commented on the vindictive nature of the divorce.

"We call them barn burners," one attorney said. "They'd rather take away the sandbox than let anyone else play in it."

A police officer familiar with domestic disputes thought he was consoling me when he said, "One scumbag microwaved the puppy in front of the kids to get back at his wife."

At home today, Pat handed me Nick's final note. *Today.* Two full years after Nick rigged a gas pipe in the basement of our townhouse and blew up our lives. Two years and four days after the letter arrived at Pat's Larchmont address.

I was too rattled to read it.

I barely had the strength to ask Pat the obvious question.

"Why did you wait so long to tell me?"

"It was one of the hardest things I've ever done."

"Why did you wait so long to show me this note?"

"Because you were barely holding it together. I worry about giving it to you even now."

"You told me you'd arrived with Sam and Grace *after* they'd cordoned off the area," I persisted. "*After* the blast."

"*I know.*"

"Why?"

"Because it would have pushed you over the edge. You got the teaching job and moved to Oregon. It wasn't the right time. I was trying to protect Sam and Grace." She wiped her eyes with the back of her hand. "I was traumatized myself."

"I'm your best friend."

"As your best friend, I thought I was making the right call. We were both a mess."

She reached for the pack of Salems she discovered wedged between the sofa cushions, then stopped herself. "All this makes me feel doubly responsible for Sam and Grace."

I looked down at the note, perfectly legible in controlled, strong capital letters. Precise as an architect's. Nick's handwriting.

I told you you'd get nothing. Not the house. Not custody of the children. Not even the dog. By the time you get this, you will be sorry you did not take me seriously and you will have nothing.

Nick's parents are leaving tomorrow. I hear Grandpa barking orders to Sam and Grace. We have had such a pleasant visit, but his tone sets me into a fit rage.

I am *sick* of sustaining their relationship with the children.

I am *done* protecting their peace at my expense.

I want to *confront* them with their son's evil madness.

I rush out of the living room, toward the kitchen, take a deep breath, and collect my resolve in front of the saloon doors I detest, along with so many other details in this rental house. Just before crashing through, I hear Pat shout, "Don't do it!"

Grandma and Grandpa look up briefly, then continue eating their lunch. Bill stands up, alarmed.

"Don't do what?" Grace wonders.

"You okay, Mom?" Sam asks.

Pat is already by his side.

I wave Nick's note in front of the grandparents, slap it on the table, but before they can read it, Bill scans its contents, murmurs *Christ!* and snatches it off the table.

"Give it to them!" I order. "And take the kids outside."

"Come with me, guys," Pat says to Sam and Grace. "Bill, talk to Juliette."

I am sitting in the living room on one of the chairs

that arrived last week. Mom and Dad left me two chairs. I have felt so homeless and rudderless that I left the chairs in storage back East, way past any measure of financial sense. I am focusing somewhat obsessively on my chair, in particular.

The one my father died in.

"It's Father's Day," I say, staring numbly at Bill.

He is sitting on the second chair, opposite me.

"I know," he says softly.

"I'm sitting in the chair he died in."

"Juliette?"

"It's a beautiful chair. A Louis XVI Bergere, probably from the time Marie Antoinette was romping around the Petit Trianon before she got her head chopped off."

"Juliette?"

"What?"

"Pat told me everything."

"Everything?"

"Yes."

"When?"

"After Wednesday's bereavement group."

I pushed myself out of the Bergere in which my father would sit, listening to my mother read to him, and stood up, weak and unsteady.

"I have no privacy," I said.

"Pat did the right thing."

"I didn't ask for your opinion."

Bill came over, squared my shoulders, and looked straight at me. "Juliette, we'll never know for sure what Nick intended."

"I think it's clear."

He folded the note and handed it back to me.

"I'm sorry, but every instinct told me to pull it away before his parents read it."

"So you're taking their side now, are you?"

"What good would it do for you, the kids, or their grandparents to revisit the very incident that has wrecked their lives too?"

"I revisit it *every fucking day*. Why shouldn't *they!?*"

"I'm certain they do, in their own way."

"Stop considering *their* feelings!"

"I'm not. I'm worried about the consequences."

"I don't need some fucking Chief of Security in my own house intercepting notes and telling me what to do."

"*Nobody* in his or her right mind would tell you what to do! I learned that the day I met you in the airport."

"And you bring that up now!?"

"I admired your independence from the outset. I just want you to think about one thing: five out of five casualties for a moment's relief is a very bad outcome. It will do a lot of permanent damage to everyone involved."

"We'll never know, will we?"

"You have the note. Pat took your car to get the kids ice cream. Their grandparents are still in the kitchen. I wanted to give you time to think about it."

He pulled me towards him and wrapped me in his arms so tightly I could smell his warmth and feel the rapid beating of his heart.

"You don't get it!" I yelled. "I'm MAD at you!" I pushed him away, as best any woman three-quarters his size and with one quarter of his strength could.

"I get it," Bill said, releasing me. "But I care about you and the kids."

"You *don't* get it! None of this is *any* of your business! Not the note, not the grandparents, not Lucas, not my kids, not my confidences to Pat. *Nothing!*"

I went too far, but I've been fighting alone for so long that the slightest kindness makes me despise any words that melt my war paint and disarm me in combat.

"They're alive, Juliette," Bill said. "What matters is that Sam and Grace are alive. *And he's not.*"

Pat returned with Sam, Grace, and our favorite terrier, Jackie. I hear Grandma Kristina asking everybody in the kitchen to turn off lights that are not immediately in use. Since their house in Yorba Linda has a Northern exposure and all their furniture is covered in plastic, their home feels like a mausoleum.

Back to screamingly boring business as usual, with Grandpa and Grandma totally oblivious to the bomb ticking in my hands.

When Bill wanders back into the kitchen, Grandpa Chola tells him that he never changes anything that is aesthetically repulsive unless it adds value to the house. Grandpa spends thousands of dollars on new windows, but the black and gold raised-velour cheetah wallpaper in the guest bathroom belongs to the same generation as the forty-year-old clothes dryer. The clothes dryer has cable hinges that snap the dryer door shut like tendons. Over the years, they've grown less tensile. Grandma Kristina taught Grace to prop a broom handle against the dryer door at a 45-degree angle to keep it shut.

I cannot wait to get out of this house.

I am grateful for the Sunday hours Lewis and Clark's law library has added to my schedule. With a passing glance at the beautiful chairs I leave behind, I now understand why people get attached to possessions, especially if they move around a lot. In my case, the chairs have become the symbol of a home that once was; the only home that might ever feel like home.

At the library, I climb past a colleague in the stairwell who asks me if I have lost weight.

"You've got to reduce your stress," she says.

She walks down, out of sight, and I want to punch her.

Shame on you, observer of the obvious.

Shame on you, picker of scabs.

Shame on you, leveler of well-intended observations with no accountability whatsoever.

I am angry with myself for allowing someone I barely know to have access to my sorrow buttons, but it's not her fault.

My body is sad, again.

Waves of grief are crashing now, slamming me against the granular sand. I put one foot forward. Any foot will do, but each time the undertow grips me with its cold, coarse hand.

Brenda was right when she told our bereavement group, "That's why we're here." The worst thing for those who grieve is to spend time with people who just don't get it. Jim gets it. He is an exquisitely sensitive soul who, despite his meticulous caregiving, will never fully recover from his partner's suicide. Macy gets it. She played us "It's Quiet Uptown" from *Hamilton*, who grieved the loss of his 19-year-old son. On a human level, the group has softened my attitudes towards, say, Mike. I will never again judge a man by virtue of Oregon's ubiquitous bald-head-with-ponytail hairstyle. Cheryl has made me accept women who spend hours on their appearance and cannot leave their houses unless they are perfectly groomed. I have come to love Ann Everything-Happens-for-a-Reason Powell, though I worry that, despite her pierced and naughty former life, her faith forces her to conclude that I will burn in hell.

In the library, I want to remind all the law students, noses burrowed in their books, that today is Father's Day.

I want to tell them to call their fathers.

When my father was ill, I called him every day.

I am already worried that Sam and Grace will be scarred for the rest of their lives by their father's death, but after Pat's confession, I live with the crushing certainty it will be so.

I prepared for my father's death my entire life. I know this sounds morbid, but when you cannot imagine the world without your father, this is what you do. Especially when you've been told your entire life that smoking causes cancer. In our car, my father would light up a cigarette, crack the window to let the smoke out, and because there were no vehicular entertainment systems, I would begin my elaborate series of calculations. Instead of word problems like *A blue car leaves Phoenix at 10:00 AM. A yellow car leaves two hours later. The blue car is driving at 55 MPH. The yellow car is driving at 70 MPH. At what time does the blue car arrive?* My childhood algebra involved a sliding scale determining how long I'd have if with him if he lived another day, another month, or another year.

We had so many false alarms with my father, including a Do-Not-Resuscitate, which my mother did not respect. That turned out to be a good thing because he lived another ten years. He lived a full seventy years after I began the calculations regarding his life span.

I am thin.
I want to go home.
I have no home.
I want my mother. I have no mother.
I want my father. I have no father.
I want a companion. I have no companion.

The next time I climb the stairs or ride an elevator with anyone who says I've lost weight and advises me, however kindly, to "Eat more nuts at regular intervals," I worry I might say fuck you and lose my job.

That's how wildly uncharitable and unpredictable I feel.

Back home in the kitchen, I hear Chola's fanatic instructions putting him in direct conflict with my children. While I was at the library, Pat and Bill took a long walk with Jackie and the children. Sam and Grace are taking responsibility for treating Jackie's allergies.

Jackie is allergic to grass. If her paws are not rinsed in a solution of one part distilled vinegar to eight parts water, she will lick them until they bleed.

The issue with Chola revolves around where to mix the solution and where to dump the vinegar.

A large foil broiling pan serves as the paw soaker. Sam and Grace rest the pan on the granite island in the kitchen, closest to the sink. With Pat's help, they lower the pan to the tile floor, soaking Jackie's paws one at a time, and dry each paw with a towel.

"Not to put foil pan on granite," Chola says.

I thought nothing could ruin granite. What's more, we're renting. This was just the beginning.

During the paw soaking stage: *Not to drip solution on tile* followed by *Not to dry paw with bath towel.*

I arrive in the kitchen just in time to see Grace so nervous she tips some of the vinegar mix on the floor. When she is obliged to use half a dozen squares of paper towel, Chola changes his tune to *There is waste.*

All five feet and three inches of Chola tower under us.

"Not to use paper," he says. He heads out to the compost heap he's started in our backyard, carrying a brown paper bag filled with banana peels and apple skins. "Use laundry room rags!"

"Where to throw paper?" Pat asks politely, waving the wad of paper towels they've already wasted. She falls naturally into Chola's syntax, hoping it might disarm him.

"To recycle."

Pat cannot help it. She has grown accustomed to the rhythm. "Where to put vinegar when done?" Pat asks Kristina after we finish soaking Jackie's paws.

"Not the sink," she says.

"Why not?" Sam asks.

"Dirty dog," Chola explains. Then he takes off to the compost bin.

"Dump it on the terrace outside," Kristina says.

"I dump," Sam says. Now he's doing it.

"Not to dump on terrace!" Chola scolds, re-entering the patio door.

"Vinegar cleans the terrace," Kristina protests.

"Vinegar kills grass."

A skirmish erupts in Bengali and German.

"Where to dump?" Sam asks. "This is really crazy, Grandpa."

"To dump in garage sink, then to lock garage door to house."

I try not to explode in front of the children, but then Kristina smiles and, thinking she will appease us all, says, "Your father would have done it this way."

I yell, *Get Out of My House.*

Two hours later, Grace pads into the living room, almost tripping over the bunny ears on her slippers. She asks if we can watch the National Geographic Special on Pompeii that Kristina gave Sam for his birthday. I am relieved. I want Sam and Grace next to me. My precious boy and my sweet girl, now ten and nine, before any smack talk, tattoos, drugs, drinking, cutting, depression, boyfriends, girlfriends, heartbreak, and car crashes. The problem is that none of us can get past the petrified dog in the documentary.

"Too sad," Grace sighs.

"He looks like our puppy," Sam says.

"We don't need this," I say. "What do you want to watch?"

"What do people watch on Father's Day?" Grace wonders.

They are usually out doing something with their father or letting their father do whatever he wants.

"Why did you kick Grandma and Grandpa out?" Sam asks.

"Because I lost my temper when Grandpa was so bossy."

"But you kicked them out after Grandma brought up Dad," Sam says. "He's their son and our father."

What am I supposed to say in my new state of congealed rage and panic for what might have been!? What's the appropriate age to tell them the truth, if at all!?

I want to scream the contents of Nick's farewell letter at the top of my lungs: "I told you you'd get nothing. Not the house. Not custody of the children. Not even the dog. By the time you get this, you'll be sorry you did not take me seriously and you will have nothing."

"Your grandparents will be here for lunch tomorrow before they leave," I tell my children, pulling them closer. "I put them up in a nice hotel with a Jacuzzi. For Father's Day."

Letter to the Afterlife

Dear Dad,

I wonder what you would think of Lucas and Bill.

Now that we can be candid about these matters, you didn't think much of Nick, did you?

Do you remember the conversation we had with cousin Walter?

You refused to use oxygen, which made your breathing more labored and your memory loss more acute. In the middle of our very intense attempt to get you to use the machine, you deliberately changed the subject to, "Let's talk about sex."

Walter said, "I'm not getting any." Then he turned to me, "Are you?" I said no.

You said something else that day, which only now resonates for me in the most profound way.

I asked you what movie you were watching. You said, "I don't know. I just collect moments."

You unwittingly described short-term memory loss in such a poetic way; yet what you said eerily applies to *my* life now.

My life is not cohering. For the past few years, I've been living as a collector of moments.

Is that the best any of us can do? What's the perspective from up there?

At times like these, the loss of your wisdom in my world is immeasurable.

I really need an answer on this.

Happy Father's Day.

Love,
Juliette

FAREWELLS

I apologized to Grandma and Grandpa before I drove them to the airport.

"We want peace," Kristina said.

Grandpa nodded. "Nice hotel," he added. "Thank you."

I said *shanti shanti shanti* as if setting an intention in Valinda's yoga class, which made them smile.

My relationship with Lucas is on hold—a cryogenic freeze.

"How long?" he asked.

"Until you're farther along with your divorce."

"Give me a break!" he groaned. "What about the Jamba Agreement?"

"Void. I need to spend more time with Sam and Grace unless they request otherwise. If they do, I'll take all four kids by myself. But *only* if it's okay with Carol."

"Your terms are extremely harsh," he said.

"And yours are extremely fluid!" I interrupted. "Why would you want to sleep with me if Grace all but convinced you I was sleeping with Pat?"

When Bill left, I did my best not to cry and thanked him for helping our family. I don't know why, but I wished he would stay longer, with his wife's postcard of the fall of Icarus. My children love him.

"When are you coming back?" they asked.

As for me, I do not know where to put my chunk of unresolved, inarticulate feelings. They usually end up somewhere between my passport and Grace's memorial rocks. That's where the fossils of feeling go—inside my top dresser drawer.

Once out the door, Bill turned back, looking worried. "I heard you screaming the other night."

I promised him I would take care of myself.

Based on the dream Bill didn't know he was referring to, I called my primary doctor and requested sleeping pills.

Nick has taken the kids for his custody day. He dropped them off at a one-day surf camp. When I pick them up, Sam is on the beach. He looks as if he's sleeping, but when I flip him over, he has a giant Band-Aid over his heart. Under it, a huge flap of skin covers an empty cavity where his heart and lungs once were. A shark has eaten them all. I pummel Nick with my fists and tell him that he killed our son. Grace sits by her brother's body, grief-stricken.

I am screaming when I wake up.

Last night, I stared at the sleeping pills my doctor prescribed. I am too scared to take them.

The doctor asked, "Are you depressed?"

I said no. I am sad.

"But are you depressed?"

I said no. "I am very sad."

They do not have a pill for sadness. He gave me an antidepressant to sleep, but pills terrify me, so I called and asked for something else because my heart hammers too rapidly when I think about the explosion on 97ᵗʰ Street and Nick's note and what might have happened to Sam and Grace.

"Are you anxious?" the doctor asked.

"Yes. Especially when I think about taking the anti-depressants."

"Are you in counseling?"

"I'm in a bereavement group."

He prescribed another pill for anxiety, which he claims will also help me sleep.

I am too anxious to take any pills.

Any thought of Pat leaving chills me to the bone.

The few times I have either been angry or have criticized Pat, she ends up surprising me with her wisdom. Not to mention her strength.

When the time comes for the departure of a friend you've known since elementary school, I say the only thing anyone can say: "I'm going to miss you." And I start to cry.

"Stop!" she commands. "We have a deal. I'm not smoking so you're not crying."

I smile feebly.

"You'll be okay. And you must continue with the group because you've been very edgy lately. You're not getting enough sex—"

"Don't trivialize—"

"Don't interrupt me—"

"I'm not—"

"AND your 44th birthday's coming up AND it's hurricane season."

It's a gift to have a friend who can articulate the anxieties hidden in the corners of my inarticulate self. She knows my history. She knows my parents. She knows my soul. It *is* hurricane season, again.

My heart is breaking for people drowning in their own homes and dogs stranded on rooftops because I am still tracking Jeanne. I think of all those who will be tracking their loved ones and looking for some outward manifestation of their presence after they are gone.

At first, I thought my mother was flying low, that she had come back to display her powers and to remind me not to forget her. But Pat mentions the latest hurricane. Someone else's mother.

"I'm going to hurricane country," Pat says.

"You're what!?"

"I'm joining the National Disaster Animal Response Team."

"Where?"

"Wherever I'm needed — Mississippi, Florida, Louisiana. People do not evacuate because of their animals. I would not either. I understand how they feel. I want to help them and rescue the animals."

"What about Bill?"

Her eyes catch mine with a look of incredulity. "Thanks to the limited number of beds during his visit," she says, "no relations were had. Either in your house and certainly not in the yurt."

I raised my palm to block any further discussion. "Too much information."

"We're on hiatus," she says, laughing at my disgust.

"Same as Lucas and me," I announce.

The next time I see Pat she will be on national television in one of those red, spandex suits rescuing dogs, babies, and the elderly, gently coaxing them into baskets suspended from helicopters.

This is why I both love and admire Pat.

Her empathy is all verb.

She will conquer death, one basket at time.

I do not tell Pat that I am irritable because I need her here, in Oregon, where she has become one of the few constants in my life.

Through Pat, my home has traveled West.

What if I can only feel at home in Oregon when Pat is here?

Juliette, Rising

Manifesto for Parents

WEST MEETS EAST

I am immersing myself in a glorious Oregon summer filled with children and long days with perfect weather.

As if begging forgiveness for the persistent rain and fog of previous seasons, Oregon summers are sunny, lush, and bug-free, with clear views of Mount St. Helens and Mount Rainier. Orchards are laden with peaches and cherries. Bushes burst with thumb-sized raspberries, staining hands and filling buckets, jams, and pies in their juicy wake.

This is my summer of repentance.

I need to recant all the stupid things I said regarding differences between the East and West coasts.

This week alone I was proven wrong for insisting that all crazy parents live out East. There are Certifiably Insane Parents from coast to coast: on playgrounds, in pools, in libraries, and in my classrooms. They live in blue states and red states alike.

Today's trip to the park served up a few examples,

beginning with a girl named Rose, who balanced on the teeter-totter with Grace. Rose is gluten-free, lactose-free, sugar-free, and dye-free. She's also television-free. Last week, the home inspector from The Churchill School told Rose's mother to disable the internet and lock up the family television for the entire summer.

Rose's mother does not believe in vaccines. So while the rest of our kids are mainlining Diphtheria, Tetanus, Pertussis, Polio, Measles, Mumps, Rubella, Hemophilus, Hepatitis B and Gardasil, Rose is a free agent.

Which is fine.

Except that Rose's mom thinks she's an immunologist.

"There's a secret study that has not been released," she whispers over the sandbox. "It definitively links vaccines to Autism."

"I believe it," one mom nodded.

"I read that too," the only dad on the playground offered.

Tough to tell whether Dad believed Rosie's mom or was simply relieved to have a point of entry. For days, he'd been waiting for the topic of conversation to progress beyond hairdressers, kitchen renovations, and math tutors.

Another mom said that *her nephew at Stanford* and *her eldest daughter at Johns Hopkins* insist that the top medical journals have put all this stuff to rest. "The author of the study lost his medical license because he falsified results."

"Ah, but *they* don't have the study! " Rosie's mother said, index finger wagging and eyes wild.

After fifteen minutes of pushing Rosie on the swing

while her mother outlined a conspiracy so vast that even the National Institute of Health was implicated, I almost shouted, "One dip in the Ganges and it's so long, Rosie!" Instead I glanced at Rosie's mom and muttered, "JFK. One gunman or two?"

Playground incidents with Rose's mom and multiple other parents make me think I need a change of air before classes start in the fall. But what sealed my conviction was Ginny's behavior at the Bellemont playground, one hour after Rose departed.

Dear Ginny, the SusieQ fundraising survivor who, at Carol's house, had given Pat a tasty recipe for Korean barbecue. Ginny had raised thousands of dollars for Palisades Elementary and designed the set for the school's fifth-grade production of *Seussical.*

When Ginny lost her temper on the playground, it was widely assumed that she was tired, pre-menstrual, peri-menopausal, or that her husband had told her to cut back on spending. At the fundraiser, Pat the Extrovert told me that Ginny was a genius and scored a perfect 800 on both SATs. After college, she married her Economics professor, who is now the Treasurer of Nike. Nowadays, *Just Do It* refers to Ginny as his favorite tax deduction. His star student appears calm, but she has really become a high-strung, corporate Nike Stepford wife. By doing so, she has raised the bar on the Stepford Wife WASP paradigm. Ginny from Seoul is a kind, brilliant, how-was-your-day dear?, don't-worry-if-the-exchange-rate-is-unfavorable-for-sportswear wife. She sounds like the Mrs. Wonderful doll Pat's husband once bought her when scouring Bed, Bath, and Beyond for an omelet pan. But *don't kid yourself*, Pat told me, *Ginny's got Mr. Nike by the balls* (at that point, Pat smiled, twisted her wrist, and clenched her fingers, as if tightening the vice). I say Ginny makes the Connecticut Stepford wives look like a relaxed bunch of disobedient slackers.

On the skate park side of the playground, Ginny unleashed her demon–in a manner hugely disproportionate to the event at hand–making the result *way* too much for any boy to process. Which is to say: I saw Ginny's son, the one with ADHD, and another boy (diagnosis unknown) arguing after an accidental collision while skating the half pipe.

I heard Ginny shout to her son, *"His father fell to his death off the north side of Mt. Hood and you're fighting in the Half-Pipe!"*

The skate park fell silent.

On any given playground, in any of the cities and towns I have both lived and taught in, I feel like crying out to all the high-strung parents, myself sometimes included, and sounding the following manifesto:

AHOY THERE! Aren't you the woman who designed that famous war memorial in college? And YOU! You're the Starbucks barista who once played Nina in The Seagull. What about you? Yes, YOU! You're the sculptor who exhibited in Berlin. And you, yes, Mr. Mom in the sandbox. Aren't you the real estate agent who was once a few strokes behind Tiger Woods in the PGA tournament? And you? The aquabelle from the

YMCA? When Pavarotti was at Aspen, didn't he single YOU out for admission to Julliard? Now you're singing the Hokey Pokey with your water aerobics students. And YOU, next to the merry-go-round that's soon-to-be-dismantled and posted as DANGEROUS. You're the government major who vowed that, one day, you would run for Senator.

Now you are all raising your children. You tell your-selves that it's much more important than your dreams or accomplishments, yet you're conflicted.

The conflict dissolves when the brilliant, witty accomplished professional at last week's dinner party turns out to be an abominable parent.

On the flip side, the best parent on the playground is stupefyingly boring.

Some of you have secret lives. Like Pat, you start emailing ex-flames in order to feel alive. Or you troll the Internet in search of a spark, a fizz, or a buzz to get you through the day.

Some of you are too tired to have a secret life and, like me, are just trying to survive.

Some of you drink too much.

Many of you are medicated.

Some of you have God, and good luck with that.

Some of you do not have God, and good luck with that too.

Your children, some of whom are my students, have been over-indulged, yet many of you are underem-ployed, mortgaged beyond your ability to pay, and worried about the soaring cost of college and health care.

Take back your lives and *let your children be*!

Two days after Pat left, I stopped to order her a massive bouquet from *Peonies, Please!* I have forgiven Pat for her decision to wait two years before telling me what happened. I know it was borne of love. I know how difficult it is to harbor a secret that festers like a boil you cannot lance.

On the gift card, I wrote my final thoughts on the subject:

Dearest Pat,
Thank you for saving my children's lives.
Love,
Juliette

After dinner, Sam, Grace, and I walked our neighborhood loop in Cook Butte Park, inadvertently giving Dolly the Llama the final word regarding my plan to leave town. As they say, it's time to take a vacation when the neighborhood llama spits in your eye. In front of my children, with a contemptuous lack of respect, immediately after feeding her an entire vine of raspberries, Dolly Llama pinned back her ears, lifted her snout, and spat in my left eye, giving me, to Sam and Grace's explosive glee, quite the bloodied appearance.

I called Macy and agreed to go to Mexico.

Mike, Ann, Jim, Cheryl, and Samantha confirmed.

We'll have to wait until autumn, given that Day of the Dead falls after Halloween, but I can arrange a few days off to span a weekend.

Pat is keen on going.

So is Bill, who will join us after his conference in Mexico City.

If Lucas proceeds with his divorce, I will thaw his cryogenic freeze and consider inviting him.

My last call was to Grandpa Chola and Kristina, who are thrilled to have Sam and Grace to themselves for a week.

19

BEREAVERS V

W e're all a bit blue without Pat in our Wednesday
group.

"Is she coming to Mexico?" Jim asked.

"Yes!" I said, which lit a circle of smiles.

"Are *you* coming to San Miguel, Brenda?" Cheryl
asked.

"Probably not," she said, softly, "but today Macy has
prepared a mini-seminar for your trip."

I wanted to know why Brenda might not come, but
we all gave our attention to the syllabus Macy was
handing out.

Day of the Dead Workshop

The Tibetan Book of the Dead
Gilgamesh: A Verse Narrative (Mason translation)
Green, Obayashi, *Death and Afterlife: Perspectives of
World Religions*
Plato, *Phaedo* (Oxford)

Tolstoy, *Death of Ivan Ilyich and Other Stories* (Penguin)
"First Law of Thermodynamics" in *Thermodynamics for Dummies*
Castaneda, Carlos, *The Teachings of Don Juan: A Yaqui Way of Knowledge*
"Day of the Dead" Readings from UNESCO and *National Geographic*

"This is hard core, Macy!" Mike said. "I haven't read a book since *Huckleberry Finn.*"

"I'm reading *Goodnight Moon* to my grandson," Cheryl said. Her eyes shifted left and right to detect any reaction that might cause her to be disinvited.

Macy tried to make the list less daunting and looked down at her index cards. "I've included readings drawn from Buddhist, Brahman, Persian, Egyptian, Jewish, and Western Classical visions of the next world."

I was intrigued, but the rest of our group met her eager expression with polite stares.

"These are *recommended* readings," Macy smiled. "Not required."

"That's a relief," Samantha sighed. "My recurring dream is the one where you walk into class and everybody's taking a test you didn't know about."

"I dream that all the time." Brenda laughed, which surprised us and lightened the mood.

After Macy finished introducing her syllabus, she welcomed comments and questions.

"The only suggestion I have," Brenda said brightly, "is to include a tactile approach to all the academic reading. It might be very therapeutic."

"That's a great idea," Ann said.

"Don't they make altars?" I asked.

"With lots of flowers?" Samantha added.

"And tequila?" Mike blurted out.

"They absolutely do *all* these things!" Macy affirmed. "And I've seen parades with women dressed in costumes and faces made up like skeletons."

"I'd like to do hair and makeup," Cheryl said.

"I can cook," Jim offered.

Mike raised his hand. "I'll do beverages."

"I'll help with the altar," I said. "I can practice on my class for Halloween."

"This is great!" Macy cried.

"I'll ask Pat if she wants to do flowers."

"We'll help!" Ann grabbed Samantha's hand and raised it, to her amusement.

Macy collapsed into her chair with an exaggerated slump. "Brenda?" she asked, looking as if the weight of her entire syllabus had lifted from her shoulders.

"Yes, Macy?"

"I *really* hope you can come."

20

PEDICURE

Summer toe-cleavage weather is here. I never *really* need my nails done, but I do need to see Mimi.

"Is Mimi from Saigon available?" I ask Tony.

"We all from Saigon," Tony says.

"Stupid American," I say.

Tony laughs a bit too enthusiastically, as if, up until now, he has not had anything but a service industry relationship with an American client. This makes him grow lighthearted before my eyes. He leads me to Mimi, and we throw our arms around each other because that's what Mimi and I do, to the confusion of other clients. Tony pats my shoulders against the back of the massage chair and fires up its most therapeutic settings.

"Television?" He smiles and points to the new flat screen.

"Sure," I say.

"Dog Show?"

"Perfect."

"How are *you*!?" Mimi smiles, peering suspiciously at the remnants of raspberry stain on my eyelashes.

She is filling the pedicure bath with hot and soapy water, the color of sapphire. "You came back!"

"Of course. I always come back."

"We talk again!"

"We always talk again."

"Kids?"

"Happy."

"Happy is good."

"Happy is very good."

I was so excited to see Mimi. Then I heard "And here's a brief preview of tonight's special: One Man's Triumph Against Cancer!"

"TONY! TURN OFF*!*" Mimi shouts. "CANCER!"

"It's okay. Just a commercial," I say, not only reassuring Mimi, but also some of the other customers registering alarm.

"Sure?" Tony asks.

"Sure," I insist.

Mimi grabs the remote and turns the volume down. "No sound will not make you sad."

I am overcome with love for this woman.

"Why do you look sad!?" She is perplexed.

"Because you're so nice, Mimi. You are a good person and I've missed you."

"Stop!" she says, her eyes brimming with tears. "Mimi can't do nails if she can't see. Pick color."

"You pick!"

"You need change?"

"Yes!"

"I pick red."

"Oh, boy."

"How is boy?"

"Which one?"

"*You* pick," she smiles cleverly.

"My son. He liked school this year."

"Very good. Next boy."

"Boyfriend?"

"Yes," she says, handing me the bottle of nail polish for inspection.

"Fuchsia Frenzy?"

"I pick *this* color for boyfriend!"

"Boyfriend needs to get divorced," I whisper, certain that at least one woman in our local salon is acquainted with either Carol or her SusieQ products.

"Boyfriend good to you?"

"Yes."

She looked up from my toes, raised one eyebrow, and pointed to my eye with a squinting expression that demanded an honest answer.

"Not the boy!" I reassure her. "Raspberry spit from a llama."

"*Mean* animal," she says, applying fuchsia to my big toe. "Boyfriend love you?"

"I'm not sure he can love someone he doesn't know that well."

"Why not?" She was genuinely puzzled. "Best time to love."

I burst out laughing and when she joined in, her brush slipped, and she had to redo my big toe.

I looked up at the television because all the women in the salon are watching *American Heroes!*

"OH, MY GOD!" I shout.

Mimi turned her head towards the screen. The other women fix their eyes on me.

Lucas is on television with his cancer survivor. *American Heroes!* is showing clips of Cycle Portland. Lucas and Carl Fortuna are cycling on the rim of Crater Lake. The shot goes to an extreme close-up of Carl. The purest expression of joy is suddenly locked in a freeze frame. Lucas says, "How 'bout that!?" Lucas starts clapping for Carl. Carl takes a modest bow. The audience is going crazy.

"Boyfriend on *American Heroes!*" I tell Mimi.

"TURN UP!" Mimi yells.

"You have remote!" Tony cries.

"Hands wet," she says.

Tony ran over and upped the volume. "Boyfriend famous!"

"Don't be modest," Lucas is saying. He wants Carl to take credit for all his good work.

But Carl does not look well. He is slumping over. Lucas sees it. "Carl?"

Carl does not respond.

"Carl! Are you okay?"

Lucas and the staff of *American Heroes!* gently place Carl on his side.

Someone in the studio shouts, "Is there a doctor in the house!?"

Lucas administers CPR and my heart beats wildly.

"Boyfriend famous!" the women in the salon shout.

Tears are streaming down Lucas's face.

Carl is dying on national television.

I leap out of the soapy water and scream and scream and nobody understands until I scream even louder,

"Carl is *dying!*" I cannot breathe. I need to get the kids. What if they are watching?

"How he die?" a manicurist asks as I fly out the door.

Tony shakes his head. "Too much exercise."

That night, I was coursing along, unconfined by my human casing. The inky blackness of what looked like outer space was filled with tiny explosions of light —as if unseen hands were holding a million Fourth of July sparklers.

I was traveling with my mother as far as I could go. I was buoyed along with my mother in spirit towards some purposeful, but unknown, unity. I was tingling—it was wonderfully pleasant—and I felt more like an electrical current or a surge of energy than a thinking, physical being. I felt certain that my mother was not suffering, and I was completely devoid of anxiety concerning my destination until she pulled away and continued on without me.

I could not reach Lucas. He usually picks up on the second ring. By the fifth, I knew he was in bad shape. He called at six in the morning, Pacific Time.

"Carl did not suffer," I said.

"I wish I knew that for sure." His voice was flat, soft, and very low.

"I do."

"How do you know?"

"I just do."

The phone went silent. I could hear the clang of free weights.

"Are you in the hotel's health club?"

"Yes."

"Does it help to work out?"

"No. I'm not working out."

"Why are you there?"

"I'm sitting on the bench press. I don't know where else to go before I fly back with Carl's body."

"Did Carl have any family members to notify?"

"He has one daughter."

"Do you want me to call her?"

"She was watching."

"Oh, God."

While Lucas was silent, I was actually missing trace elements of his hyper-positive self, which, predictably and understandably, had not withstood the strain of a tragic event, one that deeply touched his heart.

"Lucas?"

"What?"

"I'm sorry."

"OK."

"No, I mean it. I'm very, very sorry."

Poor Lucas was sniffling and trying to conceal the sound of his grief.

"I loved Carl," he said.

"I know."

"I loved him like a father."

21

STATE FAIR

As if paying tribute to Carl Fortuna, we are all showing each other uncommon degrees of patience and civility.

Lucas asks if he can join the bereavement group. He wants to join us in Mexico.

Last Wednesday, Macy's mini seminar outlined our Day of the Dead schedule. Before she turned the group over to Brenda, Jim inadvertently elicited a bit more information about Hugh Michael, simply by asking Macy if her husband, Jesse, would be joining us in Mexico. Jim's fit, slender, tidy self sat transfixed—as we all did—when Macy spoke.

"I was living in New York City getting my Masters in Library Science," she began. "I also worked as a buyer for Barney's. One week before Jesse and I married, I had dinner at a Thai restaurant in Soho with my best friend from Pratt. Each table had had its own tent. It was very Bohemian, trendy, and pretentious. I remember sitting next to a beautiful, restless man who told us he was leaving for Bangkok the next day. A skinny Finch Hatton type, from a twenties movie. All that was missing were Lindberg's aviator glasses."

"And that was Hugh Michael?" Jim asked.

"Yes."

"Sounds like my type," Jim whispered.

I patted Jim's arm in a show of support. He must be getting better if he's willing to entertain the possibility of life after Stewart.

Even Carol appears happy and healthy. At the club, she praises the drummer from the Ivory Coast for his essential contribution to the dance class Valinda recommended.

Carol thanks me for teaching the kids how to play Monopoly.

Yoga class helps me a great deal. I love it when Valinda shares sayings from her readings: "Worrying is like praying for something you *don't* want to happen." Or when she quotes Buddha: "Comparison is the thief of joy." Turns out Theodore Roosevelt said it, which intrigues me all the more.

Carol and Lucas have been co-parenting for the entire month of August. Every Sunday, they invite Sam and Grace to join Mia and Joey. This allows me to work extra days at the library, while they swim, rock climb, and visit the Oregon State Fair.

Last year, Dog Town was our favorite event. The X-Treme Air Dogs soared vast distances over water to the delight of a roaring crowd. The Art of Not Shaving came in a close second. Sam and Grace giggled as the judge scored beards for fullness (natural & fluffy), length (they measured), and style (the goatee). Mustache contestants competed in three categories: freestyle curl, big and bushy, and most artistic. Sam and Grace could not take their eyes off Most Artistic.

"He's got Slinkies made of hair shooting over his ears!" Sam cried.

At the livestock competition, we got so attached to the cows, goats, horses, chickens, and pigs that I did not want to know the answer to Grace's question. *What happens to them after the fair?*

At the law library today, Ron came in to read the newspapers and law journals, as he does every Sunday. He is my favorite Professor Emeritus of Animal Law, and someone else must love him because I know a hand-knit sweater when I see one.

Knit purl, knit purl.

I think he's a widower and I am guessing his wife knit the sweater. Every week, he wears the same cardinal-red sweater, with matching red socks.

I hope the tennis balls on his walker prevent him from skidding into despair, but today Ron collided with a woman hurling toward him with unflagging optimism at her walker's highest speed.

They crashed to the ground in slow motion.

"Oh No! *RON?*"

From behind the reference desk, I jumped up, lunged forward, then promptly tripped and fell on a curled edge in the carpet. I crawled over to the walkers that had tipped, forming a cage on top of Ron and the woman who rammed into him.

"Are you okay?" I asked.

When they did not respond, I slapped my palms on the reference desk, pushed myself up, grabbed the phone, and dialed 911.

Four hours later, Lucas dropped the kids at home. They wore cowboy hats so large they looked like a four-pack of bobbleheads.

Lucas eyed Grace and kissed me on the cheek. "You okay with that, Grace?" A smile grew on the corner of her cherry Popsicle mouth.

I had hoped the children would attend the math or spelling bee, but the pie-eating contest was writ large in blueberry on all four faces.

"What's wrong with your leg?" Lucas asked, glancing at my library injury. But he was interrupted by Mia, who could no longer contain her excitement over a plant Carol had bought each of them at the fair.

"It's a prizewinner!" she said.

"What's it called?"

"Will you be mad if I say its name?"

"Why would I be mad?"

"It's called Can of Piss."

I stared at Lucas and examined the plant more closely. Skinny stems, fanned leaves, serrated edges.

"The other name is Marry Wanda," Grace added.

"Marijuana," Sam corrected.

"My mother says it's a weed that helps sick people," Joey added.

I glowered at Lucas until he spoke.

"It was a new event," he said, sheepishly. "Sativa won first place."

Letter to the Afterlife

Dears Mom, Dad, and Grandmere,

Two days after a woman collided head-on in the law library with my favorite Octogenarian Emeritus, I visited them in the hospital.

Their minor cuts had been treated. Only their bruises remained, in marbled colors of plum and mustard.

I have been *so worried* about Ron. Every day, he wears the red sweater his wife knit. He wore it over his hospital gown.

Two concussed days after I called 911, Ron and Gilda are talking about moving in together and sharing the same caregiver.

This leaves me bewildered and hopeful.

Bewildered because I want to know, Dad:

Would you have remarried? If you *had* remarried, would you have continued to wear a sweater Mom knit you in front of *your* Gilda?

Bewildered because I want to know, Mom:

Would you have wanted Dad to remarry with or without wearing the sweater you knit him?

Hopeful and bewildered because I want to know, Grandmere:

Given that you lived until 101, do you think I might not live the rest of my life alone if I get out of the house, motor on, and smash head first into another human?

Bewildered because you know your Pascal. *Le coeur a ses raisons que le raison ne connaît point.* The heart has its reasons which reason knows nothing of.

In this case, two heads took the lead and their hearts followed.

You knit me so many beautiful sweaters, the last of which Grace still wears.

Love,
Juliette

22

A LOFT FOR LUCAS

Lucas's loft in the Pearl district is an aphrodisiac. It's walking distance from his law office. Lucas and I have not been alone for two months, though he gave me his gate code and a key. Now that I work on weekends, I devote Saturdays to Sam and Grace. By Sunday, they're sick of me and cannot wait to join Lucas, Carol, Mia, and Joey.

One hour before he was due back from work, I settled into his black Eames lounge chair. Outside his 18-foot windows, where the Fremont Bridge spans the Willamette River, the sky at dusk is cornflower blue, streaked with clouds of pink and saffron.

I must have dozed off because I awoke to a kiss on my forehead.

I stretched luxuriously, hands clasping the back of Lucas's neck. "I could get used to this place. This apartment is stunning."

"Thank you."

When I turned towards him, I felt a quivering

warmth surge through my body as I admired him from head to toe. "I don't think I've ever seen you in a suit!"

"Our case went to trial."

"Good."

"Going to trial is *never* good."

"It is for me."

"Why?"

"I like men in suits. It gives a woman something to rip off."

He laughed, sounding a bit nervous.

I was completely relaxed. No Pat, no Bill, no grandparents, no kids, no classes, no Carol. I was determined to finish what we had started outside the yurt. How hard can it be to lure a manly beast into his own lair?

"I've been meaning to tell you something," he said.

"Come tell me," I said, leading the way to the bedroom, my hand exploring a wall made of reclaimed barn wood. I jumped on the bed, kicked off my sandals, and patted the bed in invitation. The brick wall opposite me framed a river view with a tugboat pulled from an early Hopper painting. "Tell me what?" I smiled.

"If I get in that bed with you, I'll never be able to tell you."

"Even better."

"I find every inch of you irresistible," he murmured, devouring me visually, eyes resting on my feet.

"Mimi swears by Fuchsia Frenzy," I said, flirting with my toes.

The look of supplication on Lucas's face confused me. "Oh Lucas," I moaned, "if talking about the trial counts as foreplay, let's get on with it."

He laughed. "It's not about the trial," he said.

"If it's about Carol buying weed for underage children, I forgive her and will not press charges that get you disbarred."

Lucas smiled. One dimple. Very charming. It vanished in a flash.

"You're stronger than I am," he said.

"We don't *have* to arm wrestle if that's what you're worried about," I said playfully. "Now take your clothes off before I tear them off!"

"Carol was here, but it's not what you think."

What?

"Carol was here."

"I heard you."

"It's not what you think."

"What am I thinking?"

"That Carol and I might have slept together."

"That's not what I'm thinking. I have no thoughts. Only that this conversation is a massive buzzkill."

I sat up, slid to the edge of the bed, and stared at the knots in the barn wood panels.

"I know. I'm sorry. This is complicated. You're stronger than I am."

"Why do you keep saying that?" I pushed off the bed, plodded into the living room, and collapsed into the Eames chair. By now, the sky over the Fremont Bridge was a deep azure, with clouds smudged in charcoal.

I don't know how long I sat in the chair before Lucas said, "Carol wants to renew our vows."

Minute after minute passed in my state of catatonic disbelief before I muttered, "And what do you want?"

He stood behind me, pressing his hand on my shoulder.

"Tell me," I said, brusquely removing it.

"I told her I would think about it."

Tiny lights blinked like diamonds on the bridge's arch while, below, a muddied string of pearl headlights guided hundreds of commuters through the encroaching darkness.

"You're right, Lucas. It's not what I thought."

"Oh, that's such a *relief!*" he sighed. His sudden exuberance corresponded inversely to the leaden sinking of my heart.

"It's worse," I said.

I slid into my sandals, grabbed my purse, and was pulling the door open when he asked, "Can I still join the bereavement group?"

I slammed the door and ran down the hall.

He yanked it open and called after me, "Juliette!?"

I punched the elevator button.

"What about Mexico!?"

Carpe Diem

Bereavers of Mexico

The word death is not pronounced in New York, in Paris, in London, because it burns the lips. The Mexican, in contrast, is familiar with death, jokes about it, caresses it, sleeps with it, celebrates it: it is one of his favorite toys and his most steadfast love. True, there is perhaps as much fear in his attitude as in that of others, but at least death is not hidden away: he looks at it face to face with impatience, disdain or irony.

Octavio Paz, *The Labyrinth of Solitude*

You put the boom-boom into my heart.

George Michael, *"Wake Me Up Before You Go-Go"*

23

NIGHT FLIGHT

On the plane to Mexico I am watching a series about a WWII nurse who travels back in time to 17th century Scotland. She keeps a hot Scot warrior alive with her 20thcentury skills, and he sets my loins on fire. I am ashamed. Not because the Highlander has jump-started my morbid libido, but because he makes me realize that my "Best in Show" *decent, loyal, stalwart companion*, Lucas, is no more and has never been. Because Mr. Positive has chosen "living hell" for the rest of his days.

I order a Bloody Mary and flip to the music channel every time the pilot's announcement freezes my video at the show's most smoldering moments.

I am comforted by the hundreds of TV screens nestled in our cabin's digital quilt of humanity.

Macy is arguing convivially with Jesse that *Six Feet Under* is better than *Sons of Anarchy* until he applies his ear buds, retreating into a sonic cocoon with Steppenwolf.

Ann is watching *Bridesmaids*.

Mike is watching *Pulp Fiction*.

Jim is transfixed by a documentary about Princess Diana.

Cheryl is watching *Dancing with The Stars*.

Samantha is watching *Mrs. Doubtfire*.

Pat is chewing her fifteenth piece of Nicorette, enthralled by reruns of *Meerkat Manor*.

Bill is writing a speech on his laptop.

All this does not bode well for Macy's reading list or for literature in general.

I'm pretending to slog through *The Tibetan Book of the Dead* as I sip my Bloody Mary and keep a watchful eye on my Highlander.

Instead of my historic life-changing luck with compassionate seatmates, the man on the aisle to my left is snoring and my drinking buddy by the window is complaining about his wife, his job, and his kids' SAT scores. I'm impervious to his whining and to the fact that I'm in the middle seat because Bloody Mary makes me sanguine. Fortified by Frank Capra's observation *the cardinal sin is dullness,* I pivot my drinking buddy's narcotic conversation and tell him that Costco no longer sells coffins thanks to me.

"Really?" He appears almost relieved to be unstuck from the boredom of his own discourse. "My name's Jake."

"I'm Juliette."

When Jake tries to change the subject back to SAT scores, I return to the matter of coffins. "Costco used to display the silver and pink models with quilted interiors by the exit."

"I remember that!" His ruddy pink skin offsets a glorious mane of white hair. I'm guessing he's on his second marriage and I could swear I've seen him in a Cialis commercial. Instead of the usual caregiver sitting next to me, I have Jake, the Erectile Dysfunction actor look-alike: *When a moment turns romantic, why stop to take a pill?*

"Costco's products are cradle to grave," I resume, "but I persuaded management that coffins are downers, especially at the exit while my kids and I are waiting to have our receipts verified with a neon pink highlighter."

I hear Bill laugh softly in the seat behind me. When I turn back, he is smiling at me and shaking his head before finishing the speech for his conference.

Jake stares at me with a look of admiration, courtesy of his second miniature Jack Daniel's and presses the call button. "Do you want another Bloody Mary?"

"Absolutely."

It's a flight, all right—my flight from New York, the flight from Oregon, a flight from the crushing responsibility of single motherhood. A flight from Lucas Interruptus. In my euphoric state, every cell in my being sings praises to Grandpa Chola and Grandma Kristina for their loving care of Sam and Grace while I'm away.

As our flight attendant's cart approaches with in-flight snacks, Jim wipes his seat and arm rests with Lysol. Samantha and Cheryl wring their hands with Purell. Ann warns us that lettuce washed with local water in Mexico can give us "gut-busting Giardia."

Macy asks if we brought a mosquito repellant with DEET now that we're traveling to a country with confirmed cases of Zika. Pat advises me to slide the exit latch in the bathroom with my knuckle, and suddenly I am wondering if what I've been teaching my students all these years is insufficient: *Sneeze inside your elbows and wash your hands with soap and water while singing "Happy Birthday" twice.*

We have all suffered so much and here we are, at 30,000 feet, leveraging mortality by declaring war against 99.99% of all microbes. This absurd side to our bereavement group amuses me and I am happy because, for the first time in years, my flight is free of hurricanes, volcanoes, and alabaster sorrow.

24

SAN MIGUEL

T he church bells are ringing in San Miguel de Allende. Processions and altars celebrating the dead are everywhere in this colonial town of cobblestone streets, church spires, and stucco walls in shades of ochre, rust, and vermillion. The sage-blue peaks of Sierra de Guanajuato, serene in the distance, submit to the riotous colors of open-air markets below. Mounds of marigolds and buckets of gladiolus, baby's breath, and blood-red coxcombs emblematic of Day of the Dead fill the flower stands flanked by dozens of vendors selling tropical fruits, herbs, and local offerings including *epazote*, *achiote*, prickly pear, and candied pumpkin. To our unaccustomed eyes, the candy figures, sugar skulls, and *pan de muerto* (bread of the dead) are disturbing, but the collective force of their inoculating presence hastens our respect for a culture that ridicules death and praises life.

Above us, the entire village is a festive awning, strung with flags of pink, white, green, purple, orange, and aqua *papel picado,* or paper cut-outs. The scent of *copal,* a tree resin, sweetened with sage and grass, wafts from both the altars and a town square filled with families working on meticulous portraits of their loved ones, grain by grain, with seeds and colored sand.

On this first night, gleefully unattended children are running wild and shooting off firecrackers outside the Guadalupe Cemetery. Macy tells us that the children invite the spirits of the *angelitos* (little angels) back home to commence a three-day observance, terminating with the Day of the Dead on November 2.

We are trudging our luggage up the hillside and mangling a few wheels on the cobblestones in the process, only to be greeted by Dave and his peevish wife, Martha, the owners of our B&B, who clearly despise each other.

Macy booked the accommodations at the Day of the Dead Bed, Breakfast & Museo and recalls the couple from her student days in New York City. They left careers in advertising to start a business and live in the only country they could afford, Mexico. Dave is having an affair with a local woman, but he shows up dutifully every morning to help with guests because the B&B is their bread and butter.

Thanks to Macy, who met our proprietors in much happier times, Martha and Dave are allowing us to build an altar (*ofrenda*) in their courtyard. This is how the entire town and our bereavement group honors those we have lost.

Given that Pat and I are the only two bereavers who've cracked the spine of any book on Macy's syllabus, Brenda's suggestion that we consider a tactile approach to Day of the Dead serves us well.

I am in charge of designing the altar—a set of steps leading to the main flowered canopy—which, for labor intensity, surpasses Sam's upcoming Pinewood Derby race in Cub Scouts. Before leaving Oregon, I tested the structural integrity and the materials required for a smaller altar on my students, who got extra credit for learning how other cultures celebrate Halloween or All Hallows' Eve. Only Carol Schell objected to the project and Lucas, now pussy-whipped beyond recognition, apologized on her behalf at the club before I left. Carol had complained to Principal Barrow, arbitrator of *They Fuck You Up*, who overruled her objections, as did her son, Joey, my favorite Aspergerian. I was further delighted to learn that Carol, after her disappointing Bod Pod results, no longer attends Valinda's yoga class in favor of a lusty workout in the newly popular African dance and drum class.

Over breakfast the next morning, an engineer from Pittsburgh who refers to San Miguel as "the poor retiree's Tuscany" asked Martha if he could "buy some of her art." An eager smile inflated her pinched face like dough rising, erasing all wrinkles and filling it with an expression of graciousness incarnate. After ten years collecting local art, *selling* the items is the only passion she and Dave still share.

Macy urged us to buy something, *anything*, to placate Martha, who is giving us a 20% bereavers discount. Martha led us on a tour describing dozens of masks, Milagros, and Catrinas.

"Catrina is Mexico's grand dame of the Day of the Dead," Martha explains. "Her skull grins beneath a broad-brimmed hat in mockery of death."

After a twenty-five-minute lecture on back looms and cross-stitching, I asked Martha how long it took to sew one of the cotton panels she was passing around.

"That's a very American question," she said.

"HA!" Pat erupted, stunned by Martha's snipe.

I had done nothing to offend Martha and suspected that, for her, there is no greater put-down.

Martha was very attentive to the other customers and answered every one of *their* very American questions, patiently and without rancor. Determined to buy *something, anything* on behalf of Macy, I complimented Dave on a Day of the Dead crèche scene in a white box with brightly painted swinging doors and asked him how much it cost.

"That's very commercial," Martha said smugly, without bothering to turn her head in my direction. In fairness to Martha, I'm not sure she *can* turn her head: she pivots like C-3PO in Star Wars. This aside, I'm guessing that her comment is the second-biggest insult in Martha's quiver, not to mention an odd response for a woman delighting in the quick sale of identical crèches purchased by the engineer from Pittsburgh.

Her paper collection was next. Dave handed her scroll after scroll from her favorite paper artist, Salvatore Díos. After unrolling the first, she jumped smartly when a scorpion fell out and bit her on the foot.

Class dismissed!

Later that afternoon, we were so absorbed in preparing our altar that we forgot about Bill, who had arranged to visit San Miguel after delivering a paper at the global security conference in Mexico City. He had promised to arrive with punched-tin frames, given the mounting number of pictures collected by our group. And so he had. I filled my frames with a wedding picture of my mother and father and one of my grandmother in front of her hair salon on the Rue du Cherche-Midi.

Bill caught me deliberating about using the third frame for a picture of Nick with the children in Disneyland, two years before he'd started to unravel. I had kept these fossils of emotion in a paper sleeve designed for postcards, tucked under Grace's memorial rocks in my top dresser drawer. After avoiding the images for years, the mere sight of them set my heart racing and constricted my breathing. I put the Disneyland shot aside and inserted a photo of our puppy instead.

That was hard enough.

"What's the matter, honey?" Cheryl asked. The rest of our members stopped working and turned towards me.

My head was down. I was stumbling with my words.

"I just realized something," I said.

The tears were about to spill when Pat cast me a *you promised!* look in an effort to make me laugh.

I smiled, bit my lip, and resumed.

"Some of my wounds are healing."

Cheryl looked relieved, Mike nodded, Samantha smiled, and Jim's eyes misted over.

"But I'm not sure…"

Ann, Bill, and Pat waited for me to continue.

As if taking over for Brenda, Macy asked gently, "You're not sure *what?*"

"I'm not sure the others ever will."

Before I went to bed that night, I heard light footsteps and the swishing sound of what turned out to be a letter slid under my door.

Dearest Juliette,

You didn't know me growing up. I was a bit of a "dark" child. *I'm a Scorpio, for crying out loud!* My birthday is three days after Halloween.

I don't know why death has always fascinated me. Maybe because it's so taboo in the US. If I had been born in Mexico, death would have been part of my life and it probably wouldn't have intrigued me so. When I was young, I listened to morbid music and read novels about death. Now that I've grown up, I enjoy morbid music and dark autumn days. It sounds crazy, but there's nothing I like better than a dark, cold day listening to Nick Cave & the Bad Seeds or PJ Harvey or early American murder ballads like "Poor Ellen Smith" and "Pretty Polly." I made myself a "Fall" playlist that I play in my car with all of that music on it. I'd be happy to make you a copy. I just don't want to depress you.

I'm no Brenda (I'm well aware that our group has *completely* ignored my syllabus!), but I think what you said today made perfect sense.

There is a pain—so utter—
It swallows substance up—

It is my fervent hope that we all get something out of this trip to San Miguel.

Love, Macy

P.S. Sorry that Martha has turned into such a rabid bitch!

2 5

DAY OF THE INNOCENTS

The children are visiting today.

Ann is adding baby's breath and white chrysanthemums next to Jake's snowboarding photographs. The flowers symbolize the purity of children's souls or *angelitos* for November 1, *el dia de los innocentes.*

Though Brenda elected not to come, she entrusted us with a portrait of her daughter, Caroline, a joyous little sunbeam, who likely would have ended up in my classroom. Ann placed Caroline next to Jake in a *nicho*, an enclosed shrine box, on the step of the altar reserved for the children.

We took a break for Macy's bereavement seminar. She reminded us that her reading list includes selections drawn from Buddhist, Brahman, Persian, Egyptian, Jewish, and Western Classical visions of the next world. In each of them, a guide accompanies the soul and the itinerary is confined to hell.

"In *Le Songe d'Enfer*, a medieval pilgrim dines with

Pilate and Beelzebub. The menu features roast heretic and wrestlers with garlic sauce."

"Yum!" Jim cried, eliciting irreverent smiles from the rest of us.

"I know you have *not* been reading the books I recommended," Macy scolded, then added brightly, "so before we finish the altar, *you're all getting a lecture!*"

Mike and Ann groaned, but we were glad to be absolved of our reading requirements.

The reading list had triggered my nocturnal imagination.

Near the town square last night, I had seen a man behind the cemetery gate—the spitting image of Nick. I have not told anyone, and I confess to being scared. I need to know that I'm either seeing a real human who is NOT Nick and/or a returning soul who is NOT Nick. In both cases I need to know it is NOT Nick.

Macy reads from *The History of Hell* by Alice Turner. She relayed what most cultures have in common: mountains, rivers, boats, boatmen, bridges, gates with guardians, and, nine times out of ten, a tree.

"According to Paul the Apostle, unrepentant fornicators, idolaters, adulterers, homosexuals, thieves, drunkards, slanderers, swindlers, sorcerers (along with the envious, the quarrelsome, the indecent, and the greedy) will not be admitted to the Kingdom of God."

"As it should be!" Ann said. "What about paradise?"

"Paradise is more like lunch at my mother's country club in Edina, Minnesota," Macy said.

"Hell sounds *much* more appealing!" Pat's naughty laugh resurged with a vengeance.

Pat's degree from the Botanical Gardens and tips from Charles at *Peonies, Please!* made her the obvious choice for floral design. Marigolds (*cempasúchil*) are thought to attract the souls of the dead to our offerings. Given Pat's singular combination of passion and talent, I am certain her husband, Jordan, and the rest of our loved ones will not miss them. Pat's canopy over our altar is ablaze with orange blossoms and coxcombs (*targetes erecta*). Samantha works alongside Pat, adding white and blue gladiolus to the crimson coxcombs in order to honor her husband's service to our country.

Jim is baking the ceremonial bread (*pan de muerto*) and cooking his departed partner, Stew's, favorite stew.

Bill is carefully framing a single photo.

"Who's that?" I whispered to Pat.

She finished Samantha's floral flag arrangement and turned towards Bill. "His wife," Pat said softly.

"You knew her?"

"Not well," Pat said. "I was a senior in college. She was a sophomore."

"What happened?"

"Drunk driver. Head on."

Mike relishes his job arranging the beverages, while I make sure the altar won't collapse, given the dozens of bottles of water, beer, and tequila Mike's placed beside every framed picture and floral conceit. If not consumed by visiting souls, the alcohol, along with our loved ones' favorite foods, may be heartily imbibed and eaten by the living.

"I feel guilty enjoying alcohol duty," he said, addressing all of us. He did not have to remind us of his daughter's fatal heroin overdose. "Do you think I should be reassigned to something that promotes sobriety?"

"Absolutely not!" Pat said, peering between 10 by 12-inch frames of her husband grinning on a roller coaster at Six Flags and her mother holding Pat's beloved Pomeranian. "*Martinelli's* won't cut it if Jordan, Mom, and Pom-Pom show up tomorrow."

Cheryl, our makeup artist, is painting Macy's face and putting her own spin on the traditional depiction of Catrina bride by adding both discreet and discrete kidney motifs outlining Macy's mouth. "If Bob shows up, I'll forgive him for cheating on me," she says.

"He still owes you a kidney," Macy mumbled like a ventriloquist as Cheryl added the finishing touches.

Macy's altar, a marvel of conceptual art, features a framed picture of an elegant man in a linen suit nested inside a red paper-mâché convertible. Next to it, a black and white hand-knit baby blanket with matching booties lies next to a ceramic frog.

"Why the frog?" I asked.

She glanced at me; her large brown eyes now enormous in the sockets of Cheryl's ghastly makeup. With a shy smile, she confided, "It's a pre-Columbian symbol for fertility."

After we finished our glorious tribute to those we love and celebrate, I thanked Macy for her letter and vowed to listen to JULIETTE'S HAPPY MIX. Setting the tone for her entire playlist, the first track is "Rat in Mi Kitchen."

I stared at Macy's baby blanket and my mind kept replaying the phrase that had lingered with us all since Macy's first comment in our bereavement group.

I am haunted by the fact that someone I had forgotten considered me so memorable.

"Hugh Michael never forgot you," I said quietly.

"No."

"And you never forgot him?"

"Never."

I looked at Jesse in the corner of the courtyard. He was practicing down-tempo mariachi chords on his guitar. There was nothing Hugh Michael about him. He was a dark, burly, *Stop Dreaming-Start Riding* Harley biker dude. They were staying in the Dia de los Muertos suite, where Jesse read back issues of *Easyrider* and Macy prepared Day of the Dead lessons for our Bereavement Seminar.

"There's more," Macy said softly, avoiding my gaze and making sure the others were out of earshot.

"What?"

"Hugh Michael was the father of the baby I miscarried."

Oh Christ. Poor Jesse. Black leather vest, red bandana, five o'clock shadow—a husband who demonstrated exquisite sensitivity and devotion towards his wife, down to the Macy tattoo on his rippling biceps.

"Given your contribution to our altar, I'm not sure you can avoid telling Jesse," I said.

"I know," she said. "Don't Brenda me."

"I won't," I said. "I have a secret of my own."

Macy's ghoulish face returned an inquiring stare.

"Does EVERY soul return on Day of the Dead?"

"Not necessarily. Why?"

"Because…I can't believe I'm saying this…I'm actually embarrassed and terrified to ask you…"

"Don't be. You've heard an earful from me."

"I think I saw Nick!" I blurted out. "I don't know if it was *really* Nick, a figment of my imagination, or Nick from the other side."

Macy took a moment to respond.

My heart clanged like a convict banging jail bars with a spoon.

"We can't control or decide which souls return to visit," she said, then pressed her kidney-rimmed lips together thoughtfully. "But it's my understanding that those who land in hell are *not* invited."

LEONARDO

One hour before sunset on the Day of the Innocents, Pat and I wandered about the Instituto Allende and slipped into a huge room with a magnificent mural radiating movement and music.

Across the courtyard, Jesse and Macy were taking a guitar class. The Institute's class offerings reflect the interests of hundreds of foreigners who have come to retire to this artist colony. The brochure offers Salsa, cooking, Flamenco, horseback riding, music, and Spanish language classes, along with an entire curriculum devoted to art history, drawing, painting, graphic design, and multimedia sculpture.

On top of the scaffolding, a painter worked quietly, stroke after patient stroke. A portable stereo played classical music.

On the mural above us, men and women in brightly colored bathing suits were bungee jumping from a central structure resembling an elongated version of a Mayan pyramid. Lions, cellos, keyboards, and conch shells darted about the ceiling and figures swam towards us like yesteryear's underwater dancers at Waikiki.

"Muy bonita," I said to the man.

The painter turned his head and smiled. "Thank you," he replied in perfect English. He knows I'm a gringo.

"Are you the artist?" I asked.

He was wearing a gray t-shirt with cut-off sleeves. His biceps and triceps were worthy of Caravaggio's "Bacchus"— smooth, inviting, and highly defined.

"Yes," he said. He pointed to a blueprint of the mural.

His name was on it.

"*Leonardo?*" Pat laughed.

"Yes." He had a ready smile. "My parents were painters."

He picked a smaller brush to work on the headdress of a Mayan God.

"Is it hard to paint up-close when the mural needs to be seen from far away?" Pat asks.

"Yes, but Michelangelo had a much harder time," he says. "The Sistine Chapel is 20 meters high."

We are stupid tourists talking to a painter who looks like Caravaggio's god of wine. His imagination rivals the magical realism of Garcia-Marquez and he's as articulate as Carlos Fuentes.

"Your scaffold doesn't look very stable," I said.

"It is," he said.

I must not have look convinced.

"Do you want to see the mural up close?"

"Yes." Pat jumped in before Leonardo could change his mind.

"This is my best friend, Pat," I said. "My name is Juliette."

"I'll come down and help you," he said.

As he made his way down the scaffolding, slowly and carefully, Leonardo gave us a brief history of murals in San Miguel. In 1949, the great muralist Siqueiros taught American GIs at the nearby school, Bellas Artes.

By the time Leonardo stood next to Pat, I swear I could hear her hormones singing. He stood a foot taller than either of us, with dark, glossy curls. He smelled of paint and warm skin and his soulful eyes shined like burnished mahogany. If this description makes him sound as if he belongs on the cover of a romance novel, it's because he does, barring his sophistication and demonstrable talent.

"Step here," he instructed Pat, but she could not. Her legs were weakened by lust. He lifted her by the waist with his paint-splattered hands. Her mind was surely repeating the ridiculous statement I'd heard dozens of times before she married Jordan: *There comes a time in a woman's life when even syphilis is worth risking.*

I stayed below the scaffolding as Leonardo described the brush he'd chosen on whitewashed stone. He explained how he used the blueprint below to cast his figures on a larger scale.

Pat pointed to a dab of paint near his mouth, *which was not there.* She brushed her lips against his, *as if it were an accident of proximity.* Pat was so *in his face and against his body* that no man could have resisted.

My eyes traveled over the dizzy visual score of patterns in reds, blues, oranges, and browns, only to adjust to the startling image of clothes peeling off slowly—flung off and hanging like flags of surrender on the poles of the scaffolding.

I will not watch this.

I left as Ravel was playing and the sun blazed the color of a ripe persimmon.

2 7

DAY OF THE DEAD

In the middle of Martha's after-breakfast folk art lecture on our last morning in San Miguel, her husband delivered flowers with the stiffness of Lurch in The Addams Family. The Gerbera daisies were not for Martha. They were for Pat.

Martha glanced at the card. "From Leonardo," she said, smiling, then handed the bouquet to Pat.

Martha was irritated that her Day of the Dead seminar had been interrupted, but thrilled that she had stirred up something she suspected was illicit. If she could not address the Mexican woman fucking her husband, then why not expose the sexual transgressions of an American tourist. *How American,* I am surprised Martha did not say. *Doesn't every American woman travel to have an affair?*

Ann and Cheryl eyed each other but kept silent.

Samantha bore a look of mild disapproval.

Mike cast his eyes downward, respecting Pat's privacy.

Macy did not react because I had told her about Pat's encounter.

A smile crept along Jim's mouth until Bill entered the room.

We listened in silence as Martha showed us examples from her costume collection, representing over sixty indigenous Indian groups. She announced that any of the pieces she had shown us, or that we have seen in her *museo,* were for sale.

"How American," I said.

I was seething with anger towards Pat, but Martha provided an easy target.

"Excuse me?"

"I'm sorry. I meant to say, *How vulgar.*"

"What do you mean?"

"The very *idea* of *selling* art for profit from your *museo!*"

I glared at Pat, stood up, and headed back to my room.

Five minutes later, Pat appeared at my door.

"*How could you!?*" I exploded. "What's *wrong* with you!?"

"It's really none of your business, Juliette."

"Actually, it is."

"Why is that?"

"You seduced Leonardo, right in front of me."

"You left before—"

"That's not the point."

"What's your point?"

"Did you tell Bill?"

"Why would I tell Bill?"

"Answer the question."

"I did not tell Bill. Now answer *my* question. Why *should* I tell Bill?"

"I consider Bill a friend, so knowing something Bill hasn't been told makes it awkward for me."

"Why would *I* tell him?"

"Because it's the right thing to do."

"Nothing will come of me and Leonardo."

"Wouldn't you want to know if your boyfriend had slept with someone else?"

"Bill's not my boyfriend."

"Does *he* know that?"

"You know we were on the rocks before Oregon and his visit shattered us further. I've been training with my animal rescue team. He's been working and probably missing you a lot—"

"I'm not so sure about that—"

"I'm stating the obvious!" Pat threw her arms up in exasperation and knocked Martha's favorite milagro cross off the wall. She picked it up and slapped the cross back on its exposed nail. "What's going on with you and Lucas anyway?"

"Lucas is renewing his vows."

"*What?*"

"He's back with Carol."

"*Why?*"

"I don't know. He said he wasn't strong enough to go through what I went through."

"Nobody is," she said somberly.

"I love his kids," I said.

"Me too, but Lucas is not for you, Juliette."

"Don't hurt him, Pat."

"Lucas!?"

"No, Bill."

"I never have, and I never will," she said. "And what-ever happens…" She pulled a tissue out of her new Frida Kahlo gift shop purse, "I love you both."

Pat almost never cries. I get in trouble if I do.

She stared out my window. The stark noon sun had bleached San Miguel's church domes in a chalky yellow light.

There was nothing more to say, which had never kept either of us from talking.

"By the way," Pat said, turning towards me. She gave her eyes a single dab before stuffing the tissue back in her purse. "This might not be the time to bring this up."

"Then *don't!*" I warned.

If Pat revisited *any* sensitive subject on my list of grievances—the Leonardo incident or the withholding of Nick's note—she was bound to unleash that spicy chi that takes me by surprise, no matter how many times I've forgiven her.

She caught my eye with a mischievous look.

"*What?*"

"Leonardo wants to paint you."

She clapped her hands over her mouth to stifle a nervous laugh, but her eyes were still merry.

Later that afternoon, Macy swept into Martha's court-yard with a brilliant smile on her face. "Don't you just *love* Mexico!?"

She wore a brightly embroidered Mexican dress and with no makeup, she looked ten years younger.

For our final seminar, Macy introduced another

philosophical death nugget for discussion: "Death in the natural order is a random, unremarkable event. Without meaning."

Of all Macy's topics, this one alone jarred us. To die of natural causes, for humans, means to die in old age. For animals, ninety percent of whom die before maturity, it means to die young.

Pat whipped out her black Moleskin and wrote with her Day of the Dead souvenir pencil:

Death
in the natural order
is a random, unremarkable event.
Without meaning.

Brenda's not here to patrol us, so we let Pat write. I was happy she was writing again.

Bill wandered into the courtyard. I asked him what he made of the statement.

"Which statement?"

Death in the natural order is a random, unremarkable event. Without meaning.

"It makes me think of Lucas," he said, explaining to our group that Lucas was an environmental lawyer and naturalist. "In the wild, Lucas witnesses death every day. Yet the recent death of his friend, Carl Fortuna, hit him very hard."

"What does the statement mean to *you*?" Macy asked Bill.

"As the husband of a wife who died in what I guess

could be called the human version of a random, unremarkable event…" He paused and struggled to regain control. "My wife died in a car accident—a statistical anomaly…" His voice broke. "It's unbearable."

"I'm so sorry, Bill." Macy said. "I had no idea."

Murmurs of sympathy emanated from each and every bereaver. I grabbed his right hand and squeezed it; Pat had instinctively grabbed his left. We both let go as he sat down between us.

Jesse dropped by, but he wanted no part of our bereavement group. He asked for directions to Bellas Artes for his last guitar lesson.

"Jesse," Macy said, "what do you make of what we've been discussing?"

"What have you been discussing?"

"The idea that…actually, it's a fact that *Death in the natural order is a random, unremarkable event. Without meaning.* We are having difficulty accepting death without meaning."

"Death gives life meaning," Jesse said.

"Has Lucas been a different man since Carl's death?" Pat asked me.

"Yes, but I don't want to talk about Lucas," I muttered.

Jim asked Macy, "What meaning do you think there was in Hugh Michael's death?"

"*Carpe Diem,*" Macy said. "Seize the day."

"Who's Hugh Michael?" Jesse asked.

"I'll tell you later, honey." Macy looked at me. "I promise."

Jesse left after Macy gave him directions and Jim

raised his index finger, signaling to Macy that he had something to say.

"I have a story that might relate to our topic."

"I'm sure we'd all love to hear it," Macy said.

"But first, I have to know why you're not wearing makeup," Jim grinned.

"Fair enough," Macy smiled. "Before leaving San Miguel, I have to tell Jesse about Hugh Michael."

"I was wondering if that was Hugh Michael on the altar," Mike said.

"It is. And I removed my makeup to face myself and my obligation to tell my husband under the harsh and cleansing light of the Mexican sun."

"You look like a beautiful 17-year-old." Jim laughed.

"So true," Cheryl added.

"Put your makeup back on so we all don't look like your parents!" Ann said, adding, "I'm not sure you have to tell Jesse *everything* if it's in the past. It might hurt him."

"I agree," Pat said.

"So do I," Bill said. "Even though I know nothing about it."

"I love you guys," Macy said, tears welling up. "I'm so glad you all agreed to come."

"Now for the topic I've avoided sharing by asking Macy about her makeup," Jim said.

"We're even, Jim," Macy smiled. "I just noticed that your nails are not buffed."

Jim smiled and looked down at his dry, coarse hands. "Stew and I had a cat," he began. "We loved the cat and were sick with worry when the cat disappeared for days."

"My cat does that all the time," Ann said. "We got a dog."

Jim nodded. "Our cat's name was Doggie. We were sure the coyotes had killed her."

I could feel the collective mood shift to one of unease as we worried that Doggie's story might be an example of death in the natural world.

"Pictures of lost cats were posted on poles all over our neighborhood," Jim said. "Five cats. Not one recovered." He ran his thumb over his ridged nails, then looked up. "But that's *not* what happened to Doggie."

Pat sighed with relief. "So the coyotes *didn't* get her?"

"Our neighbors confessed that Doggie was living at their house."

"So far so good," Bill said.

"I like you, Bill," Jim said. "I just need to say that because I wish you had joined our group earlier."

"Thanks, Jim," Bill said. "I'm sorry if I interrupted."

"Not to worry. Anyway, the point is that our neighbors didn't want to tell us that Doggie was living with them."

"Why?" Cheryl asked.

"They thought we'd be mad."

"But you were *relieved*," Samantha said.

"Not exactly."

"Why not?" Macy asked.

"Because our neighbors wanted to keep our cat."

"Oh, boy," Mike said.

"Cats are so *fucking* disloyal!" Pat cried. "Sorry, everybody. You know I love animals, but cats *are* animals—wild ones. Sorry, Jim."

"It's okay. Anyway, our neighbors loved Doggie. But we did too. Especially Stew."

Even I felt compelled to interject. "You all know I lost a puppy and numerous family members and was embroiled in a horrific custody battle. The fact that Doggie did not fall victim to a coyote makes me very, very happy."

"That would be the *rational* response," Jim said. "Except Stew was angry. Very angry."

"I'm getting nervous," Cheryl said.

"Stew screamed at our neighbors. *We raised that cat and you took her away from us!* Our neighbors yelled back, *Doggie's made her choice and we love her too.*"

"Five cats in your neighborhood had been killed by coyotes," Macy said. "Were you able to focus on the fact that Doggie was alive and well?"

"No," Jim said. "That's why I brought this up. We are talking about random deaths in nature and that's exactly what was happening in our neighborhood. The food chain was at work: Coyotes 5; Cats 0. It's not that Stew and I wanted her dead. It's more that Stew needed to *own* Doggie in order to love her.'"

"So did your neighbors," Ann said.

"That's not love," Macy whispered.

"Exactly," Jim said, with an honesty that chilled us.

"But it's human," Bill added.

Jim stood up and placed our group's last picture on the altar. Stew was holding a large calico cat.

None of us asked what had happened to Doggie.

Not even Pat.

Before dinner, Pat handed me an envelope marked For Your Eyes ONLY. Inside was a poem she had been writing for the past few weeks. She apologized for subjecting me to her affair with Leonardo. With her poem, I'm guessing that she wanted me to see Philippe Petit as her kindred spirit, given his own high-altitude affirmation of life.

Carpe Diem, New York City
(after Philippe Petit's magical walk from the North to South Towers of the World Trade Center in 1974)

After the New York City Police
removed your handcuffs
and asked you *"Why?"*
You replied, "That's such an American question!"

What's also American is that
after you had walked
in midair
from the North to the South tower
A woman offered herself to you—
A complete stranger!
To celebrate (and consummate)
your death-defying
affirmation of life—
O, high-wire artist
O, intoxicating *funambule!*

The rest of us
(cowards beneath you)
watched you dance
and genuflect—
smiling in the face of what we saw
as certain death.

In September of 2001
when death came to so many
from the very same towers
at the same heart-stopping height–
Hand in hand, one couple lept
(but, this time, we wept)
because there is never a net
though it's only human to hope
(past hope)
it will appear.

28

BILL

I finished packing and heard a knock on my door.

I did not want to speak to anyone.

I did not want to have dinner with my bereavers.

I hate goodbyes and Last Suppers *never* end well.

I cannot wait to see my children, but re-entry to Oregon will be difficult. I will reenter my life as a penguin.

After the documentary, *March of the Penguins*, Sam, Grace, and I felt betrayed. As children, we are fed happy images of penguins, dapper in their tuxedos.

"Too sad," Sam said.

"*Happy Feet* was better," Grace added.

"Glad I'm not a penguin." *Real life*, I wanted to say.

The movie was a hit. Parents can relate: they take turns marching miles for food, regurgitating the food, sitting on the egg, marching back for more food, spitting it up, and divorcing with the statistical regularity of penguins once their "eggs" are hatched.

The life of a penguin, devoid of passion, awaits me in Oregon.

I cracked the door and was startled to see Bill.

"Did you eat?" he asked, with a disarming smile. "Pat fell asleep reading the first book on Macy's reading list."

"I'm not hungry," I said. *And The Tibetan Book of the Dead is not the only reason Pat's tired.*

Bill was wearing a suit and tie.

I do not tell him that Pat seduced a painter named Leonardo on the scaffolding at the Instituto Allende. I ask him why he is wearing a suit.

"The last of my clean clothes," he said. "You look glum. Let me buy you dinner."

I left the door ajar and fell onto my bed in a fetal position. "I'm a mess," I said. "Today was intense and I'm going to miss everybody."

He closed the door behind him and sat by my side, with a window view of the church of San Miguel.

"I'll miss everybody too," he said.

"What are you staring at?"

"You have the most amazing eyes. They're gold with flecks of nutmeg and a .3-millimeter black ink circumference."

"Amber," I said. "Your eyes are always changing color."

"Blue," he said, "according to my various IDs."

"I'm VERY mad at Pat, but I don't want to talk about it."

"Is that what's bothering you?"

"I'm *extremely* mad at Pat, but I'm also sad that she's leaving again."

"Have you told her you were mad?"

"Yes."

"Have you told her why you were mad?"

"OH, *very* much so."

"Have you told her that you're going to miss her?"

"No."

"Why?"

"Because I'll cry, and she'll start smoking. We have a deal."

"That's a good deal!"

"As far as missing her…" I borrowed a phrase from Pat. "Why state the obvious?"

Bill shook his head. "Sometimes it's important to state the obvious."

Bill's solid presence was so comforting that I drifted off and when I awoke, the church's fiery yellow dome was a cooler shade of saffron.

"Fajitas are the medicine of choice for the despondent," Bill said softly. He is so good-natured I had trouble concealing my smile. My unconscious mind had allowed him to hold me because it was aware of two things Bill might not know: Pat had moved on and Lucas Kumbaya was back with Carol Vesuvius.

"I'm hungry," he persisted. "And speaking of mud-eaters, where's Lucas? I thought he was coming."

"I don't want to talk about Lucas." I flipped on my stomach and buried my face in the Atomic pillow embroidered with festive farm images.

"I'm relieved that we don't have to talk about Lucas.

It's tough for any man—let's call the man an "interested party"—to listen to a woman pine for another man."

I rolled over, propped my elbow up on the festive pillow, and squinted at him with curiosity.

He laughed outright.

"What's so funny!?" I fumed, reaching for one of the 3 remaining pillows, this one with a paradise motif, and whacked him soundly on the left side of his head.

"Christ!" he cried, grabbing my wrist to prevent another swipe. "Maybe you should look in the mirror to see what amused me before drawing your weapon," he said.

I rolled onto my knees, craned my neck, and peered into the punched tin and tile mirror. My eyes were swollen, and my hair was sticking in all directions—the spitting image of Macavity in *Cats*. A donkey from the Otomic pillow had imprinted itself on my cheek, which, compared to the rest of my appearance, was a marked improvement.

"I told you I was a mess."

"Nonsense," he said. "The donkey on your cheek suits you *perfectly*."

Fighting words. I grabbed two of the remaining pillows, but Bill's reflexes were too quick; he straddled my waist and grabbed my wrists to batten them down. I squirmed beneath him.

"Getting back to my initial proposal," he said, scanning the room for any other weapons I might use against him. "My fajita offer still stands."

"I don't *want* fajitas."

"Duck with molé negro?"

"No!"

"Fine! Order whatever you want."

My heels kicked the back of his buttocks so forcefully that his lapis blue eyes widened in confusion and, gentleman that he is, he promptly released me.

"Seriously, Juliette. I'm starving to death." He pushed off the bed and headed for the door.

I sat up as abruptly as Joan of Arc hearing voices. "I understand," I said. "I'm hungry too. Let me wash my face, comb my hair, fix your tie, and I'll be ready." I waved him over. "Tie first," I said, eyeing the pathetic sight of myself yet again in the mirror.

He scanned over my unkempt hair, puffy eyes, wrinkled clothes. As if afraid of starting another battle, he choked back a laugh, converting it to a half smile, and dutifully approached me so I could fix his tie. After a long pause, during which I found myself drawn to his crisp summer suit and the manly body it concealed, I pulled his tie and drew him toward me.

"Do you even *know* how to fix a tie?"

"I'm very manual." I said, "I'll figure it out." I undid the tie and whipped it off his neck.

"What are you doing?" he protested.

"I'm figuring it out," I smiled. "How was your conference?"

"Excellent, actually."

"Excellent," I said. "By the way, Lucas has reconciled with Carol."

Bill was taken aback, doubly so after I pressed my mouth fully against his lips and pried his mouth open with my thumb.

He bit my thumb, gently, as I tossed his tie to the floor. I started to unbutton his shirt, charmed by the finger-maiming level of starch that was slowing me down.

"Hey, Juliette?"

I ignored him and ripped off his shirt. The buttons bounced off the terracotta tiles.

"You ruined my best shirt!"

"Collateral damage; the TSA took my pliers. Jesus, why all the starch!?"

"To keep women from ripping my clothes off! So far it's been *extremely* effective."

He kept moving his head to catch my eyes with his blazing blues.

"Seriously, *Juliette*?"

"What?"

"At this point, protocol and human decency require me to ask if what we're doing is consensual, especially since your breakup with Lucas is recent."

I ran my hand slowly over his smooth, strong shoulder and traced his muscles down the splendid torso that had almost bruised my hand when I'd smacked him in the abs on Bod Pod day.

"Two hundred percent consensual."

My hand rested on his thigh before it moved inquisitively to the most tangibly responsive part of him. I rubbed slowly with my unrelenting palm.

"What about you?"

"God, yes," he whispered. "You have immense power over me."

"Immense, indeed," I murmured, feeling his granite presentation as I unbuckled his leather belt.

His eyes met mine, clear as a cyan pool in the dying rays of the sun. "Permission to undress?" he whispered.

I nodded, though I happened to be wearing my least accessible outfit. The blouse I'd purchased at the San Miguel market had as many buttons as a Victorian camisole, along with an off-the-shoulder string lassoing it to my arms. Bill painstakingly explored the cotton fortress like a wondrous voyager, fingering his way through. He cupped my breasts and planted a lingering kiss on each one, then pinched my nipples with his teeth until each one hardened like snapdragons pulled off a vine. A melting, coursing pulse overtook my entire body with increasing insistence.

I drew his pants over his firm, rounded buttocks, dropping them to the floor. Before I knew it, he had deftly slipped off all remaining articles of clothing between us.

His fiery licks coaxed me open. Tongue and sheathe, his hard digs pried me wide and responsive as a sea anemone.

"Oh!" I cried.

"Did I hurt you!?" He stopped suddenly.

"No!" I gasped. My breath grew shorter, faster, and sounded more guttural with each of his crafty improvisations.

"I'm going to explode," I moaned.

"Explode," he murmured. I could feel his mouth smiling between my thighs. He deepened his entry with another penetrating jab, only to stop again.

"Where did you go?" I issued a stinging slap to his buttocks like a jockey with her crop.

"Right here." His tongue tickled the inside of my ear

and he kneaded my sides with his strong, warm hands, traveling down, kissing my throat, my breasts, my navel, teasing every inch of my quivering body until he returned to the root of all pleasure and cupped my hips, muscling his way deep inside the throbbing marsh he'd pounded back to life.

I felt the mounting waves of unbearably shimmering pleasure and pulled him towards me, thrusting him deeper until we were sealed as one.

He wove his hands into mine and pinned them above my head.

I kissed him, *Now*.

And so began our gasping, grasping, rocking, rushing, crushing, convulsive, smashing-wet, blood-pounding down and dirty sex.

When we came up for air, he fell back on the bed and exhaled deeply while I shuddered with pleasure. He tipped me on my side, folded one arm around my waist, and stroked my hair in silence.

A few minutes later, he said very quietly, "I'm going to miss you, Juliette."

I hid my face and wiped my eyes with the only vestige of bedding I could find.

He inched his torso over me, dipped his head, and investigated my face with a worried look.

"Was it *that* bad!?"

I turned to face him, flipped him on his back, and nestled my head between his arm and chest. I could hear his heart pounding and feel his breath moving up and down his abdomen.

"Hardly," I said.

"So what's wrong?"

"What are we going to do?" I asked.

"About what?"

About our mind-crushing, soul-binding lovemaking, you idiot! I wanted to shout.

"Why the tears?" His face bore a sad look of resignation, which morphed into a quizzical impishness. "You *are* thinking of Lucas."

"Oh, for God's sake. No!" I laughed so hard that I slid off his body.

Outside, the moon hung, half-eclipsed, by the night's drowsy eyelid.

We could hear the distant noises of parades and dancing from Day of the Dead celebrations.

I ran my fingers through the wavy crop of chestnut hair untamed by his grown-out military cut.

"Aren't we too old for this?"

"No," he said. "Not since you took me to Valinda's class."

"I didn't *take* you!"

"You're right. It was the only way I could get away with lying next to you in the dark."

I drew his head back down to my chest and planted a kiss on his forehead.

"You never answered my question," I said, as he nestled back to my breast without an inch of waning daylight between us. "What are we going to do?'"

"I don't know, but I know one thing." He lifted my arm, kissed my palm, then clasped and folded my fists between his hands as if sealing a vow.

"There's no turning back, Juliette."

I lay with his solemn words, which took my breath away. Something gnawed at me and it took me a while to figure out what it was. When I did, I knew it was perhaps not an appropriate time to bring up the subject.

"You don't have to respond," I said, scanning his face for any sign of disturbance. "I just wanted to tell you how sorry I am about your wife and how lucky she was to have you."

"I was lucky to have *her*," he said.

"You both looked so happy in the picture. Life is…" I was too choked up to continue.

"Unfair," he said, licking an active roller off my cheek. "But I don't know anybody who comes through life unscathed. I can't relate to people who haven't suffered."

That night, we ordered fajitas, *juevos a la Mexicana,* and a bottle of tequila from Martha, though room service was not provided by her bed and breakfast. I could hear the irritation in her voice when Bill requested the duck with mole negro, which was confirmed both by her stiff entrance and her sniffing disapproval when she delivered dinner with her back to us, placing it on the small tile desk under the window.

"*Really*, Juliette. Room service?" Bill whispered, with feigned derision. "How *American.*"

I muffled a fit of giggles. "Martha, please leave the tray on the bed," I instructed in the staccato voice from forties movies: *Henrietta, you may draw my bath.*

Martha pivoted mechanically and dropped the tray

on the bed, averting her eyes from the sheets, pillows, and quilt that formed a mountainous shrine to our tempestuous lovemaking. I sighed and thanked Martha with the languorous, indulgent smile of a woman who had been properly bedded.

Holiday Season

I have been in Sorrow's kitchen and licked out all the pots. Then I have stood on the peaky mountain wrapped in rainbows, with a harp and a sword in my hands.

Zora Neale Hurston, *Dust Tracks on a Road*

29

BEREAVERS VI

I have been cleaning with a vengeance. I would rather eat ant trays than scrub floors, so I wonder what has come over me. Dusting the family pictures on our bookcase conjures up answers. Grace turns nine this month and my parents will not be at her party. They will never be at her party. I am grateful for Grandma Kristina and Grandpa Chola, who are here for Grace as they were for Sam, but their son and her father will never again be at her party.

Death makes me hate the holidays. Every one of them is perfectly calibrated to torture the lonely. I remind myself that I am not the only person tortured on holidays. You either don't have a parent, have an abusive parent, are looking for your biological parent, despise the parent you've been given, are seeking some connection with the one you already have, or spend all day explaining that you have either two fathers or two mothers who love each other very much.

The *Oxford Book of Death* offers no solace.

Non-fiction books are either too earnest or humorless.

Nothing helps—not the irritable last hours of Ivan Ilyich, not St. Therese of Lisieux, not C.S. Lewis.

Macy's HAPPY MIX is too strange.

Everyone in our community supports society's cruelty to grievers.

They ask:

What are you doing for Father's Day?

What are you doing for Mother's Day?

Where will you spend Christmas?

The absolute worst is New Year's Day.

Everything is closed. No distractions. I try to be optimistic about the New Year, but I am stuck in time, for what feels like The Day of Perpetual Torture. It really doesn't matter what year it is.

Except this year I miss Bill.

Today is our last bereavement group of the year. Brenda told us she had not been ready to go to Mexico. She read from a letter she has been writing ever since she lost her daughter.

My Precious Caroline,

When I lost you, all my hopes and dreams for you died, along with those of your father, grand-parents, teachers, and friends.

You were our future.

The moment we laid eyes on your sonogram, we felt a wondrous love. We readied our house with cribs, jolly jumpers, highchairs, bouncy seats, and baby swings. We opened a savings account in your name.

Now, we comb through all the things you loved: I SPY, *Magic School Bus*, Play-Doh, lanyards, sparkle paints, Disney movies, Halloween costumes, ballet outfits, soccer team photos, and Jewel Sticker Stories.

At night we have nothing to put in your backpack. No lunch with Goldfish or gummy snacks. No box of Kleenex requested by your teacher.

Our garage is a monument to your enthusiasms: skis, bicycles, Boogie Boards, fishbowls, beach balls, soccer balls, and ice skates.

Before your father and I start the car, we stare at each other as if we have nowhere important to go. No dance practice, choir practice, piano lesson, or birthday party.

All the hours we cheered for your soccer team and clapped for your performances. All the nights we read you to sleep.

We have too much time we *don't need* and *don't want* without you.

Brenda's voice broke. She stopped reading.

On the Day of the Innocents in San Miguel, we had celebrated Caroline's life. We were all picturing the tow-headed girl with huge gray eyes and a smile that radiated joy.

Macy and Samantha cried quietly. Jim wept. Cheryl dabbed her eyes and passed around the travel pack of tissues she'd pulled from her purse.

Mike wailed, "This is fucking torture, Brenda!" He stood up, folded her into a bear hug, then, drunk with misery, he stumbled back to his chair.

"May I add to your letter?" Ann asked gently.

Brenda nodded, her eyes fixed vacantly on the letter in her lap.

"Geiger counters, fire trucks, cement mixers, and back hoes," Ann said. "Tonka trucks, Naruto, Pokemon, chess sets, and half a dozen skateboards."

I covered my face with my hands and felt Macy pry a tissue between my fingers.

Mike picked up from there. "Ski lessons, guitar lessons, gymnastics, and that fucking carnivorous plant kit that never produced a single Venus flytrap!"

Pat would have laughed, and Mike would have loved that: We all missed her terribly.

I knew what Pat would say to Brenda, so I said it for her.

"Brenda?"

She looked up, wan and bleary-eyed.

"You have been taking very good care of us. Now you need to take care of yourself and let us help you."

At the Lewis & Clark law library later that afternoon, I looked forward to seeing Ron and his new bride, Gilda, but my heart was still stuck in our bereavement group. I was overcome by the empathetic bravery it took for Ann and Mike to add to Brenda's letter. At the same time, I was filled with dread. I prayed I would never have to utter Thomas the Tank Engine, Curious George, baseball mitts, Snap Circuit kits, and NASA or, for Grace, Kaya, soccer cleats, state fairs, and Philip Larkin. At the end of the day, we are all teachers and parents. When we execute our jobs perfectly, we still feel like abject failures if we lose a single child—our own or someone else's.

During my break, I called Pat, but she was busy with her last week of rescue training before the holidays. The last time we spoke I was prepared for a long conversation about Bill after I opened with, "This is awkward," but she cut me off.

"Not for me," she said. "I love you both. It's a perfect match. If you don't believe me, ask Sam and Grace."

I left a message for Bill, the gist of which was a resounding *I love you.*

Throughout today's group, Bill's words had rushed back to me. *They're alive, Juliette. What matters is that Sam and Grace are alive.*

Later that evening, Grandma and Grandpa were sitting on the battered velour couch in our living room. In spots, it was pink and bare as a baboon's butt.

"We put the children to bed," Grandpa said, pausing *Mrs. Doubtfire*. "Sam is sneaking on the computer."

"So is Grace," Kristina said, shrugging her shoulders. "We tried."

"It's okay," I smiled. "They don't have school tomorrow, and I set the internet to disconnect at 10 p.m."

Kristina fingered the crushed parts of the sofa, as if trying to recover the events which, over the years, had made each impression.

I offered to make them an omelet, but they had eaten. I was exhausted anyway. Kristina looked at Grandpa as if asking for permission to talk.

Grandpa nodded.

"He had problems," she said.

"*Sam?* What happened?"

"Nick," Grandpa corrected.

"Sit down, please," Kristina said, patting the spot on the sofa next to her.

I sat down perfunctorily, numb with fear. His name had never crossed their lips.

"Nick had problems," Kristina repeated.

Minutes passed. They were comfortable with the passage of time.

"We were happy when he married you," Grandpa said. His voice was low and grave. "We thought he would get better."

30

EPITAPH

B ack East, my parents have been underground for more than two years, and I am ashamed to admit they don't have a tombstone. It's still too painful to return to their grave, but this is not the Tomb of the Unknown Soldier. I cannot leave them unmarked. Even my grandmother has a gravestone. My mother made sure of that, not knowing that she herself would need a headstone four months later.

I have hired Jean-Claude Gaulois to tutor my children in French. While Sam and Grace await their lesson, they watch *DockDogs* on ESPN . The dogs leap over quadrangles of water. Bella's owner throws a decoy and the sports announcer cries *Bella has caught some big air!* This last jump puts the black lab nose-to-nose with Willard, a golden retriever.

"WOAH!" my children shout. Willard has tied things up.

Macy, my resident expert on the literature of death, is here to help me pick epitaphs. She likes "Together

Again" (Gracie Allen and George Burns). I ask her why she's so cheerful performing a task that does not normally elicit exuberance and she cannot contain herself. "I'm pregnant!"

"Oh, Macy!" I cried. "I'm so happy for you and Jesse!"

After three attempts, we finally reached Pat online in Louisiana. I handed Macy my laptop: "First trimester and all's well!"

Sam and Grace marched in, said hi to Pat, announced Willard's victory, and congratulated Macy. Pointing at the General Electric service truck across the street, they asked in unison, "What about *We Bring Good Things to Life*"?

Pat told Macy that my father had worked for the company Thomas Edison founded. "What about Edison's last words?" Pat said.

Sam stuck his head in front of my laptop's camera. "What were they?" he asked.

"*It's very beautiful over there*," Pat said.

I want to find an epitaph my parents would like—one that's simple, beautiful, and consoling—yet I love the element of whimsy Sam and Grace introduced.

I toy with a line from the Marquis de Favras. My father used to write letters to *The New York Times* and various other newspapers to correct their grammar. In 1790, the radicals of the French Revolution caught Favras as he plotted to help Louis XVI escape. Favras was convicted of treason. After a two-month trial, he was handed his official death sentence by the court clerk. As he was led to the scaffold, Favras said (and presumably these were his last words), "I see that you have made three spelling mistakes."

Jean-Claude arrived in time to cast a vote for the French royalist. "I love Favras! And because you are including me in a process normally considered very personal," he added, "How about *Toujours Ensembles*?" (Always Together). More suitable for an oenologist, he threw in *"Enivrez-vous"* ("Be Always Drunken", from Baudelaire).

Later that afternoon, I went to the only Catholic church in Bellemont to light a few candles. The church of St. Francis was made of wood, with soaring beams— the kind of church in which guitars take the place of organs. "We're a modern church," the priest said. Not a candle to be found.

When I got home, Sam and Grace wanted to buy stars online.

For $49.95, we named a real star in the heavens for Jeanne and named a second twinkly piece of real estate after my father, Louis. Then I saw the cluster option. For $109.99, we put them together and included my grandmother, Paulette.

I tell my children that it does not seem possible, in our lifetime, to run out of stars or suns or moons or galaxies—which might give us some notion of eternity, the infinite, or even the divine.

"We need another $20 for Dad," they said, "and $10 more for the puppy."

"Should we get Dad his own star?" Grace asked.

"No, I want him to be with the rest of our family," Sam said.

Letter to the Afterlife

Dearest Mother,
I started this book to honor your memory.

Between the beginning and this ending, a lot of living has been going on, some of which I would have been more inhibited about pursuing if you and Dad were around.

My heart is still breaking and, some days, your daily absence is huge enough to feel palpable. It's like a huge, sad tumor made of air. I am learning how to negotiate life with this enormous presence of vacancy.

On the days I am tracking you less often, I worry that if I *don't* think of you, you will vanish altogether.

I am proud to have completed something devoted entirely to your memory.

This is your book, conceived in graphite, etched in granite, and stored on a cloud.

Thanks to Sam and Grace, we now have a family star cluster. Your grandson was so excited he shouted *a bit too eagerly*, "We can always add Mom later!"

All my love,
Juliette

P.S. Tell Dad and Grandmere that I am in love with a man named Bill Cunningham and I am certain they would approve.

EPILOGUE

Jean-Claude Gaulois opened a wine store in the Pearl District and emcees an open-mike wine tasting on Friday nights. He tutors Sam and Grace every Sunday.

Valinda and the Chi Master started an online Wellness and Meditation brand, though Valinda still teaches one class to her disciples at our club.

Lucas and Carol gave birth to a beautiful black boy in May and the family has joined another health club. They are planning a family trip to Guatemala next year to celebrate Mia's birthday.

Pat passed her certification test. She arrived with Leonardo on Mother's Day, carrying a rescue puppy for Sam and Grace.

Rosie demanded that her mother pull her out of The Churchill School and Oregon State Law required that she receive Diphtheria/Tetanus/Pertussis (DTaP), Polio, Varicella (chickenpox), MMR or Measles, Mumps, Rubella, Hepatitis B, and Hepatitis A vaccines. Grace reports Rosie is much happier at Palisades.

Grandma Kristina and Grandpa Chola are far more relaxed after confiding in me. After all these years, I am grateful and relieved that they stated something many parents would be loath to reveal.

Our Wednesday bereavement group died of natural causes, but we meet often to commemorate those we've lost; or to rejoice, in the case of Macy's little girl, the gift of new life.

Bill came to visit on New Year's Day and has not left.

ABOUT THE AUTHOR

Fabienne Marsh is the author of four novels and numerous works of non-fiction. Her film credits have appeared on dozens of documentary films and she has taught writing at both Johns Hopkins University and the University of Minnesota.

Marsh grew up in Edgemont, New York, the daughter of a French mother and a father of Irish-English descent. At Williams College, she studied with John Gardner and took a double major in English and political science. After a five-year stint with the documentary unit at ABC News, during which she enrolled in the Columbia University Writer's Program under a Woolrich Fellowship, Marsh won a journalism fellowship and studied international relations at The London School of Economics. Upon her return to the States, Marsh worked on television documentaries, while publishing her critically-acclaimed novels, *Long Distances* and *The Moralist of the Alphabet Streets*, followed by her third novel, *Single, White, Cave Man.*

Marsh has served as a writer-consultant for Nickelodeon, HBO, Turner Broadcasting and Public Broadcasting (WNET and WETA). Her lighter works of nonfiction include *Dave'sWorld*, with co-author Michael Cader about David Letterman, and the coffee-table book, *Saturday Night Live: The First Twenty Years*, for which Marsh interviewed Candice Bergen, Steve Martin, Chris Rock, and other cast members.

Marsh's freelance articles have appeared in The New York Times, the Chicago Tribune, The Economist, the International Herald Tribune, Southbay magazine and Poetry Review (London). Her radio essays aired on MPR's "Marketplace" and WHYY. Marsh has taught literature and creative writing at Loyola (Baltimore) and for three years, she served as the Journalism Advisor for the Chadwick School in California.

Marsh is currently living in the South Bay of Los Angeles and has recently completed her fourth novel, *Juliette, Rising.*

APR 2 3 2021

Made in the USA
Middletown, DE
10 April 2021